"Would you let me hold her so you can eat?"

"You're sure?" The blue of Eli's eyes darkened with emotion. "Even though you said goodbye to me?"

"I was upset that night," Brianna answered honestly. "Your daughter is so precious, Eli. Of course I want to hold her, but I'll try not to wake her."

"Don't worry about it." He walked over and placed Libby in her arms.

The motion caused her eyelids to flutter open. Her blue eyes were so much like her father's.

"Hi, darling. Do you remember me? I'm Brianna."

The little girl put her arms around her neck and clung to her. Brianna held her against her heart and felt her breathe. "I'm so glad you're feeling better." She rocked her back and forth, loving the feel of those arms holding on to her.

Though he sported a slight beard and looked exhausted, Eli stood there watching them with a sweet expression on his rugged face. "I do believe you're the reason she's suddenly acting normal."

Brianna smiled up at him. "Her daddy is all the medicine she needs."

Dear Reader,

I'm crazy about the gem shows on TV! I love looking at all the beautiful stones. It's a holdover from my childhood when I read a story in my school reader about a boy named Patrick who came across a cache of jewels in the forest hidden by the fairies. The colored drawing portrayed him kneeling in front of this gorgeous, sparkling pile of gems. It captured my imagination like you can't believe. From that point on, I loved looking at jewels in stores. When I was in England and saw the crown jewels, especially the orb and scepter, I was entranced.

So...when I was looking for a new location for my next four-book cowboy series, I came across the Sapphire Mountains of Montana. Immediately I knew my series would be called Sapphire Mountain Cowboys. It was the place where I wanted to stage my story, especially when I learned that a huge amount of gorgeous sapphires were taken out of the mines there. As you might guess, my exceptional hero, Eli Clayton, falls in love and has big plans for a large blue sapphire found in the Clayton mine. It has been cut in a heart-shaped design. You'll have to read *A Valentine for the Cowboy* to learn the details.

Enjoy!

Rebecca Winters

PS: I was born on Valentine's Day, so no one knows better than I how exciting it is to have a birthday on that day!

A VALENTINE
FOR THE COWBOY

———

REBECCA WINTERS

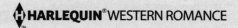

Recycling programs
for this product may
not exist in your area.

ISBN-13: 978-0-373-75742-8

A Valentine for the Cowboy

Copyright © 2017 by Rebecca Winters

Printed in U.S.A.

HARLEQUIN®
™ www.Harlequin.com

Rebecca Winters, whose family of four children has now swelled to include five beautiful grandchildren, lives in Salt Lake City, Utah, in the land of the Rocky Mountains. With canyons and high alpine meadows full of wildflowers, she never runs out of places to explore. They, plus her favorite vacation spots in Europe, often end up as backgrounds for her romance novels, because writing is her passion, along with her family and church.

Rebecca loves to hear from readers. If you wish to email her, please visit her website, cleanromances.com.

Books by Rebecca Winters

Harlequin Western Romance

Lone Star Lawmen

The Texas Ranger's Bride
The Texas Ranger's Nanny
The Texas Ranger's Family
Her Texas Ranger Hero

Hitting Rocks Cowboys

In a Cowboy's Arms
A Cowboy's Heart
The New Cowboy
A Montana Cowboy

Daddy Dude Ranch

The Wyoming Cowboy
Home to Wyoming
Her Wyoming Hero

Visit the Author Profile page
at Harlequin.com for more titles.

Dedicated to my fantastic parents, who somehow managed that I would be born on Valentine's Day. They made that birthday special for me all the years that they were alive. What a blessing!

Chapter One

"Hey, Brianna—I keep telling you I wish you'd come home. You could *never* be in the way. When you said you wanted to stay with Aunt Joanne and Uncle Clark in Montana, I thought you'd only be gone a few weeks. It's now been six months!"

"I know." She looked at the Cattlemen's Association calendar on the wall. It was already the twenty-seventh of December. "But I've been doing well here working for them. I like being busy and was afraid if I came home for the holidays, I'd be overwhelmed with memories and I can't deal with that yet."

The car crash that had killed her beloved parents seven months ago had been so devastating that Brianna was amazed she'd survived this long.

"I hear you," he said in a mournful voice, "but I want you to realize that Carol and I miss you more than anything."

"I feel the same way." But Doug, her elder brother, who was as blond as she was and sounded like their father, had only been married to his longtime girlfriend a few months before their parents had been killed. They were now running their parents' fruit farm in Marysville, California, and making a success of it. This early in their marriage they shouldn't have to worry about Brianna. Not when they'd had so much responsibility thrust on them.

The aunt and uncle she adored and who'd been so close to their family had never been able to have children. They'd begged her to come and live with them for a while.

"If you stay away any longer, you'll probably forget you have an older brother." He was twenty-seven to her twenty-three.

"Don't be silly. I love you to death and promise to fly home soon." The nearest airport was in Missoula, a half hour away from Stevensville. An hour if the roads in midwinter were bad. According to her uncle, this winter hadn't hit them too hard and business had been good. Today was a beautiful day with a lot of sun that had brought in the customers.

Four or five times a year since she was a little girl, Brianna had come to Montana with her family to visit her aunt and uncle. They often took in a rodeo because her father and uncle once did bull riding themselves and Brianna loved it. In fact the three of them were going to the Stevensville rodeo tonight. While she stood there swamped by sweet memories, she heard the front door open. It was closing time, but she hadn't locked up yet.

"Doug? I've got a customer. I promise to phone you next week and we'll have a good talk after I'm off work. Give my love to Carol."

"Will do. Talk to you later, sis."

Brianna hung up. An attractive male, probably in his late twenties, had just come into Frosts' Western Saddlery, one of Stevensville's oldest and most well-known stores. They sold everything cowboys and cowgirls could possibly need. A lot of men young and old came in all the time, but she'd never seen this guy before. He had light brown hair and wore a gray North Face half-dome hoodie and jeans.

His hazel eyes twinkled as they fastened on her. "I can see you're new here. Where's Clark?"

"He left for home ten minutes ago." Their ranch house was only a mile away. "What's your name? If it's an important matter, I'll call him and tell him you're here."

"I'm Roce Clayton, but please don't bother him."

That name caught her attention in a hurry. "One of the legendary Claytons?" The Clayton Ranch was one of the oldest and most famous ranches in the Bitterroot Valley. It lay between the Bitterroot and Sapphire Mountains outside Stevensville. What a co-incidence! Brianna was planning to drive there later to visit the Sapphire Mine Gem Shop owned by the Clayton family.

"Well, now, that all depends." His smile made her chuckle. "What's your name?"

"Brianna Frost."

She could hear his mind working. "You're Clark's niece!"

"Yes. How did you know?"

"I'm a vet. I've taken care of their dog, Taffy, for the last year."

"Aha. So that's where I've heard your name."

"He just called me to take a look at her. I'm afraid her hip is bad."

Brianna loved that dog. "She's getting worse."

"It's a shame. You know, whenever I make a visit, all he talks about is you and your brother."

"You poor man."

"Not at all. I heard about your parents' death. Clark took losing his brother very hard. I can only imagine the pain you've suffered. I'm so sorry."

His sincerity touched her. "Thank you." She cleared her throat. "I understand your father passed a little while ago, too. My uncle really misses him. It couldn't have been an easy time for your family, either."

"You're right about that. He died thirteen months ago. Thank Heaven my mother is still alive. My older brother Wymon is head of the ranch now, but, between you and me, we'd all fall apart without her."

Tears stung her eyes. "I know what you mean. You're lucky to have her."

"That's for sure, but I don't see her often enough."

"Why is that?"

"I work at an animal hospital in Missoula and only come home when I can take an odd weekend off." He gave her a half smile. "Anyway, I just thought I'd drop in to buy a pair of driving gloves while I'm on my way to the ranch."

"For yourself or someone else?"

"For me." He gave her the size. "My old ones are falling apart. Maybe I'll pick up a pair for my mom, too."

"We've got some great gloves." She walked him over to a display case and showed him several styles. He found the gloves he wanted and went back to the counter to pay for them.

After handing him the bag she said, "If you're going to the ranch, could I follow you? I've never been there and I want to visit your family's gem shop. Uncle Clark wants to give my aunt a gift for their wedding anniversary coming up next week. I told him she'd love a ring. I'd like to see what's available."

"Then you're welcome to trail me."

"Thank you so much. Let me just grab my jacket and purse from the back, then I'll meet you in front."

After she'd locked up, Brianna stepped outside and was greeted by clear blue skies, the temperature hovering around a chilly thirty-four degrees. She climbed into the Ford pickup her uncle let her drive. It helped that the sun had melted the ice on the windshield. Roce Clayton waved to her from his black Escalade and she followed him down the snow-packed road in the direction of the ranch.

He seemed like a great guy—it was too bad she wasn't attracted to him. While Roce had been buying his gloves, she'd noticed he didn't wear a ring. With a smile like his and his classic good looks, she figured he wouldn't be single much longer. Her brother had been like that. Attractive and sweet. Carol had fallen for him in high school. Brianna hadn't found that kind of connection with anyone yet.

She'd had a series of boyfriends in college, but she'd never been in love before. Not really. Her feelings toward the guys she'd dated had never been that strong. Brianna's mom had told her, "When you meet the right one, you won't have to wonder. You'll know it in every atom of your body."

She let out a sigh and followed the car in front of her around a curve in the road. Light glinted off the magnificent snow-capped mountains studded with pines. It really was a spectacular drive. Five more miles and they reached the entrance to the Clayton Ranch with its tall arch of antlers. Somewhere on their property was the entrance to an old sapphire mine.

Her uncle had told her stories about the first two Clayton brothers, who'd hailed from Lancashire, England. In the late 1800s they worked and slaved to bring a big herd of Texan longhorn cattle to Montana, where they bought land and built their business into one of the most successful ranches on the western side of the state. They also bought mining rights as sapphires had been discovered throughout these mountains. Apparently Elias, the elder of the two brothers, neither married nor had children, so the legacy came through Wymon. The present-day Clayton brothers all had old English names to preserve their heritage, Roce being one of them.

She tried to remember the other brothers' names but failed. She thought she would ask Roce when they arrived at the ranch. The Sapphire Mountains were looming closer, and she figured they mustn't be far now.

THE SECTION OF the Sapphire Mountains known as Gem Mountain was also called the "Quiet Giant" because it had produced over 180 million carats of sapphires over 120 years, yet it didn't receive a lot of publicity. According to Brianna's uncle, people in the early part of the twentieth century used to dig for larger sapphires that could be polished and sold for a lot of money. The fractured stones were sold for industrial purposes and many of them were shipped to Switzerland to be turned into watch bearings.

After World War II the rock hounds came. The Claytons had sapphire gravel brought out of their mine and they opened their own gem shop. People would sift through the material and often find a special sapphire to buy. Today you could still visit the mine, but it was much easier to shop at the store owned and run by Roce's mother, where you could see the sapphires on display.

Brianna's thoughts were still concentrated on finding the perfect sapphire for her aunt when the large, two-story ranch house sitting at the base of one of the foothills came into view. When the Escalade pulled up in front, Brianna slowed to a stop and waited for Roce. He got out and walked over to her.

She lowered the window. "Your ranch is fabulous."

"It is to me because it's home."

Home. How would it be to go back to Marysville

and find her parents there? She could only hope that one day she'd stop hurting so badly.

"I'll go inside and find Mom. Be right back."

"It's okay. I'm not in a rush."

She expected to wait a while, but to her surprise Roce came back out in no time. "I just spoke to the housekeeper, Solana. It seems Mom decided to take advantage of this warm break in the weather and went up to the gem shop this afternoon."

Brianna smiled. "I guess thirty-four degrees in Montana in December *is* warm."

He grinned back. "Yup. Why don't you get in my car? I'll drive you and bring you back here. It'll be easier than giving you directions."

"If you're sure, that would be great."

"Of course."

She climbed down from the cab and got into the passenger side of his car. Her aunt and uncle had been so wonderful to her that she really hoped to find a stone that her uncle would be excited about to give his wife.

AFTER WORKING ALL day in the winter pasture, Eli took care of his horse and then left the barn and drove his blue rattletrap of a truck down to his house to shower and change his clothes. He made himself a couple of peanut butter sandwiches before leaving to pick up his daughter at the main ranch house. The ranch foreman, Luis, and several stockmen waved to him from a distance.

When Eli pulled up to the house, he saw an unfamiliar Ford pickup truck parked in front. It could be someone here to talk business with Wymon, except his brother's truck wasn't around. Neither was the Land Rover.

Anxious to give his little girl a hug, he hurried inside, but no one seemed to be about. There weren't any voices coming from the front office. No patter of little feet. He walked through the foyer and down the hall to the kitchen where he found the dark-haired housekeeper at the sink, washing vegetables.

"Solana? Whose truck is out in front?"

She looked over her shoulder. "Roce came home from Missoula and brought a woman with him. I suppose they've gone up to the gem shop in his car."

Whoa.

Maybe his brother had finally found the perfect woman to settle down with. He'd certainly had his share of girlfriends over the years. Roce had probably invited her to tonight's rodeo. Their brother Toly and his partner, Mills, were competing in the team roping event. "Did you meet her?"

"No."

"Where's Mom?"

"She took Libby to the shop with her. They'll be back soon."

He checked his watch. "She'll need to be since we're leaving for the rodeo in an hour and a half. Are you sure it won't put you out to watch Libby while we're gone?"

"Of course not. I love her."

"She loves you, Solana. Even so, I'm trying to find

the right person to take care of her so you and Mom don't have to shoulder the whole load. Libby's my responsibility after all."

"Stop your worrying," the housekeeper said. "We're happy to help."

"And I appreciate it," Eli said. "But I want you to know that I am looking." Now that his daughter was fourteen months old, she was a real handful. His mother insisted that taking care of Libby helped her deal with her husband's death, but it was still hard work and no one knew that better than Eli. "I'll drive up there and relieve her." He grabbed a bottle of water from the fridge to wash down the sandwiches and went back out to his truck.

After starting the engine, he took off up the road past the barn and outbuildings, but a great weight had descended on him. It wasn't fair for his mother to be taking care of Libby when she'd already raised four sons and had found fulfillment running the gem shop. Though he was trying to be a good father and pull his weight on the ranch, his guilt about the impossible situation was growing heavier with every passing day.

Sadness filled Eli's soul when he thought about his ex-wife, who'd become too ill to raise their daughter and had suffered a nervous breakdown. He'd loved Tessa and they'd had a good marriage. Yet after the baby was born, she'd become a different person. He fought hard to keep their love alive and would have done anything to make their marriage work.

When she'd said she wanted a divorce, he was shattered. The word itself—the whole painful thought of it—was the last thing he'd wanted to hear, but she didn't relent. It left him with no choice since her happiness had to come first. Paying for it had been costly.

He'd been saving money to pay for a woman to watch Libby. But it couldn't be just any woman. She'd have to be a saint! Could there ever be a replacement for Eli's mother? She was so wonderful with Libby, but it pained him that she couldn't spend more time at the gem shop she owned and loved while she was taking care of his daughter.

Before he reached the shop at the base of the mountain, he spotted Roce's Escalade parked in front next to his mother's Land Rover. He shut off the engine and climbed down, eager to take his little girl back to his house. She'd become his whole world.

As he opened the shop door and felt the warmth envelop him, he saw his precious Libby in the arms of a shapely woman in a light-colored sweater and jeans standing at the counter talking to his mother. She had to be Roce's girlfriend. There was no sign of his brother. Where was he?

Eli couldn't help staring. She had the kind of otherworldly gossamer hair he'd always longed to run his hands through. While he was still mesmerized by her, Libby saw him and called out, "Dada!" His brunette daughter started squirming to get to him.

He moved toward her as the woman turned around. Eli was almost blinded by eyes that were the same deep blue as some of the sapphires in his mother's shop. Libby reached for him and hugged him around the neck, breaking the spell that had held him captive.

"All the light bulbs have been replaced." Roce's voice came from the back room. He emerged and gave their mother a kiss. "Hey, bro." He smiled at Eli. "How are things going? Libby gets bigger and cuter every time I see her."

"I think so, too," he muttered, caught totally off guard. "She's my little cowgirl. Aren't you, sweetie?" After kissing her cheek, he eyed his mother. "Thanks, Mom. Just so you know, I'm headed home. If you're going to the rodeo with us, you need to be at the ranch in an hour." On that note, he headed for the door.

"Wait—don't forget this." His mother held up Libby's little parka.

He'd forgotten because he couldn't get out of there fast enough. Eli reached for the coat and put it on his daughter, aware of the younger woman's engaging smile.

"Bye-bye, Libby."

He suffered another shock because his daughter smiled back. "Bye."

Their exchange trapped the air in his lungs because Libby had never said that word before. Once back at the truck, he fastened his daughter in the car seat and started down the mountain road.

Eli knew he'd been rude to leave like that. *So* rude, in fact, that he hadn't even answered his brother's question about his welfare. But the sight of Libby in that woman's arms had jolted him. Normally his daughter wasn't comfortable with strangers, but she'd seemed perfectly content with this one just now.

As for Eli, he hadn't been involved with another

woman since meeting Tessa two and a half years ago. After a quick marriage and early pregnancy followed by a divorce, he'd devoted his life to Libby and had lost all interest in women, or so he'd thought.

So what in the hell had just happened to him? He'd stood there helplessly assessing her attributes as if he'd never seen a beautiful woman before. What made it worse was the fact that she was Roce's girlfriend.

Had his brother noticed Eli's behavior?

Of course he had! Roce didn't miss anything.

Damn and damn.

BRIANNA TRIED TO concentrate on the reason why she'd come to the shop in the first place, but the arrival of the little girl's gorgeous daddy had brought a tension she couldn't shake. Was it anger she'd felt as he pulled his daughter away from her?

She'd offered to hold her while Mrs. Clayton showed her the sapphires. The little fourteen-month-old was so adorable and Brianna had loved entertaining her. Yet the father had seemed anything but pleased. Brianna wasn't exactly pleased, either.

Not only had she felt a strong and immediate physical attraction to Roce's brother—something that rarely happened to her just by looking at a man—it wasn't until he was putting the parka on his daughter that she noticed he wore a wedding ring.

Life played mean tricks on you. Roce Clayton didn't wear a ring, but he hadn't caused her heart to race when they looked at each other.

Time to snap out of it, Brianna.

After a moment's hesitation, she chose the stone she loved the most from one of the trays. "Can you set this dark pink sapphire aside? My uncle will come to pick out the setting he wants and pay for it then. Will you be open Monday evening? He can be here by six. Their anniversary is on Wednesday."

"We'll take care of all of it on Monday," Mrs. Clayton said, smiling kindly. Brianna could see where her two sons got their good looks. They all bore a resemblance to each other.

The pretty dark-blond widow whose short hair was cut in a becoming style also possessed a charming nature and was wonderful with her granddaughter. She turned to Roce. "I'm ready to go if you are."

"See you back at the house, Mom." After he gave Libby a hug, they walked out to his car and started down the mountain.

"Thank you so much for bringing me here. I found exactly what I wanted for my uncle. Your mother is so knowledgeable about these stones. It was fascinating listening to her."

"Dad had the gem shop built for her to run. What started out as a hobby turned into a career for her. Over the years she's made quite a name for herself. She brings in business from all over the country."

"With your father gone, I'm assuming it has become even more important. She's a lovely woman and her granddaughter clearly adores her."

He nodded. "Dad fell for her the first time he saw her."

"That's so wonderful. It was the same with my brother and his wife. Love at first sight."

He grinned at her. "I would say it doesn't exist, but then I see it happen to other people all the time."

Brianna was thinking the exact same thing. Her mind flickered back to Roce's brooding brother. Did he have a fairy-tale love story, as well? When they reached the ranch house and Roce pulled up next to her truck, she opened the door. "Thanks for driving me up there. I really appreciate it."

"It was my pleasure. I guess you heard us talking about the rodeo. Have you ever been to one?"

"Yes, actually. Plenty of times. My father and uncle were both bull riders years ago. We're going to the arena tonight."

"Then you'll see our baby brother, Toly, and his partner, Mills, competing in the team roping event."

"Uncle Clark said one of the Clayton boys would be in the lineup. We'll be rooting for them."

"I have to be there early to check over their horses. Why don't you and your family join ours in the bleachers? We'll save seats for you down in front."

"That's very generous of you. Thank you."

"Good."

"One thing, though, Roce. Can you please not mention that I went to your ranch today, and ask your brother and mother to do the same? Uncle Clark wants to keep the ring a secret."

He winked. "Understood."

She jumped down. "Thanks again for everything. See you there."

On the drive to Stevensville she wondered if she was crazy to have accepted his invitation. It couldn't be construed as a date since it was meant for the whole family. That was the problem. His brother would be there, the *married* one with the piercing blue eyes. The *angry* one with the darling daughter. Brianna didn't even know his name. Would his wife be there? Roce had provided no explanation for his behavior. Of course it was none of her business.

An hour later she and her aunt and uncle bought their tickets and made their way through the crowd inside the noisy enclosed arena. Excitement was high because Stevensville's favorite son was competing. Brianna scanned the bleachers down in front and picked out Roce's mother right away. There were empty seats on either side of her.

"Brianna?"

She turned her head. "Hi, Lindsay!" Her married friend worked at the bookstore a block away from the saddlery. They often ate lunch together during the week.

"Come on," her uncle murmured. "The parade is beginning. Let's just sit here for now."

She waved to her friend and followed her aunt and uncle down a nearby aisle. The three of them found seats and watched the horses prance around, ridden by the contestants carrying flags. Brianna loved the fanfare and the smell of the horses, but tonight she was distracted and kept her eyes on Mrs. Clayton. After the national anthem had been sung by a local country singer, she watched three tall, hard-muscled men file into the row and sit next to their mother.

Brianna had never seen three such handsome brothers. Brianna couldn't distinguish who was who in their Stetsons.

A minute later one of them stood and began walking up the stairs. As he approached, she could tell it was Roce. She waved to him and he walked over and shook hands with Uncle Clark and Aunt Joanne. "I'm glad you're here. Why don't you all come with me?"

Her uncle and Roce talked about Taffy's condition as they followed Roce to where his family was sitting. The poor dog was on her last legs, a sad fact of life that couldn't be ignored.

The saddle bronc riding event was announced. Everyone shook hands quickly before it started. Brianna's aunt and uncle knew all of the Claytons and greeted Roce's mother warmly, calling her Alberta.

Roce explained that he'd been to the saddlery earlier in the day to buy gloves and had met Brianna there.

He went on to introduce Brianna to his brothers Wymon and Eli. But the first contestant was out of the box, stalling the conversation for the time being. Brianna sat on the end next to her aunt, but, instead of concentrating on the rodeo, her thoughts were on the brother named Eli, who'd come without his wife.

Roce was conventionally handsome and Wymon, whom Roce had introduced as the eldest brother, had light gray eyes that stood out in striking contrast to his black hair. Still, it was Eli with his rugged dark looks and his black Stetson who made Brianna's pulse quicken. She silently cursed herself for always being attracted to the bad-boy type.

All rodeos thrilled a crowd and this one was no exception. She held her breath throughout the team roping event and whooped and hollered along with the rest of Stevensville when the best time went to Toly and his partner. The celebrating went on for a long time. According to her uncle, the Clayton family hoped Toly and Mills would go to the Pro Rodeo National Championship in Las Vegas next December.

Brianna could only imagine how much the Claytons missed their father at a time like this. Her own parents would have loved this rodeo, too. She wished they were here and missed them terribly. It was especially hard not to have her mom to talk to after what had happened at the gem shop earlier that day. Her awareness of the man sitting five seats away had dominated her thoughts all night.

She was relieved when the barrel racing ended and the winners received their gold buckles. With the rodeo over, everyone got up to head outside. While her uncle stood talking to Roce, Brianna put an arm through her aunt's. "I'll walk out to the car with you."

"He could be a while. Clark lives for nights like this."

"Dad did, too."

Brianna thought they'd evaded any more socializing and was happy when they reached the car and got in. But then along came her uncle with Roce, who walked around the front of the car and knocked on the window. She asked her aunt to turn on the ignition so she could lower it.

He smiled down at her. "You got out of there too fast for me to say good-night."

"Thank you for allowing us to sit with your family. It made the whole evening that much more exciting and we're so proud of your brother."

"It was fun. Too bad I have to get back to Missoula tomorrow. But when I come to visit again, I'll drop by the saddlery. If you're not busy, maybe we could go out to dinner."

"That would be great," she said, blushing.

"Good. I'll look forward to it."

After they drove off, her uncle glanced at her through the rearview mirror. "I do believe you've made a conquest of Roce Clayton."

"I don't think so, Uncle Clark," she said. "If he were truly interested, he would have asked for my phone number and said he would call me. He was just being nice because he lost his father and knows I lost mine."

Her uncle made a turn and followed a line of cars out onto the highway. "The girls around here have been after him for years. He was a great bull rider before he gave it up to go to veterinary school. Can you honestly tell me you're not the slightest bit interested in him?" he teased.

Her uncle knew she'd spent time with him earlier in the day, but he'd made assumptions that were way off base. "Yes," she said without hesitation. The memory of Eli was constantly before her eyes.

"That sounded definite," her aunt said.

"He's a fine man, honey."

"Clark—" her aunt cautioned him. "Leave the poor girl alone."

Brianna leaned forward and patted his shoulder. "You sounded like Dad just now and I love you for it. But as Mom once told me, when I meet the right man for me, I won't have to question it. I'll know he's the one." *But please, don't let him be a married man...*

"Of course you will," her aunt concurred.

"I'm just saying you couldn't do any finer than a Clayton."

Both she and her aunt laughed the rest of the way home.

Chapter Two

Eli drove to the ranch house with Wymon and their mother. He raced upstairs so he could take his daughter home, but Solana stopped him at the door to the bedroom.

"She's asleep. Don't wake her up now. I'll watch her tonight and you can come get her in the morning. You've been going nonstop for months. It's time you had a break."

He reached out and hugged her. "You already gave me one. Toly won another gold buckle tonight. He's racking them up! Thanks so much for watching Libby so we could all be there to support him."

"She's a little angel. Luis and I couldn't have children so there are no grandchildren. Libby fills a hole in my heart."

He nodded. "She's my whole heart."

"I know. Luis and I promise to take good care of her tonight."

"You don't have to tell me that." He shoved the cowboy hat back on his head. "If you're sure you're okay, I'll be over at seven to fix her breakfast."

"Why don't you sleep in?"

"Even if I want to, I'm always awake by six anyway."

"You're still too young to be saying things like that."

"Didn't you know I've aged since my divorce?" he teased, but there was a kernel of truth in what he'd said.

Solana's expression sobered. "I *do* know," she murmured. "So does your mom. Now go on home and relax."

Eli walked back down the hall to the stairs. He could hear voices coming from the living room and found Roce talking privately with their mother. They appeared almost secretive. Wymon must have gone home to his own ranch house, and Toly would probably be out celebrating late with Mills after their win.

"You two are so quiet that I'm beginning to wonder if something's going on that I don't know about."

His mom stared at him in surprise. "Why would you say that?"

"I don't know. When I walked into the ranch house earlier today, I learned you were up at the gem store with Libby. A strange truck was outside." He eyed Roce. "Solana told me you'd brought a girl home with you. When I drove up there, I found you and a woman I've never seen before holding my daughter while picking out a stone." A drop-dead gorgeous woman. "Are you with me so far?"

Roce broke into a grin. "Mom? Shall we tell him?"

She nudged him. "Oh, don't be such a terrible tease."

Somehow Eli didn't feel like laughing. Anything but.

His mom moved toward him. "Eli? What's eating at you?"

"I just wondered if you and that girl might be serious."

Roce's eyes narrowed. After a silence he said, "Not yet, bro, but I have to admit she's a hottie."

"Oh, for Heaven's sake, Roce—" their mother chastised him. "Brianna Frost came up to the shop to pick out a stone for her uncle. He plans to give his wife a ring for an anniversary present. Roce had been to the saddlery for some gloves. She asked if she could follow him to the ranch because she'd never been to the shop before."

"Maybe you didn't know I've been caring for her uncle's dog, Taffy," Roce chimed in. "To be friendly, I asked her if she and her family would like to join ours to watch the rodeo. Nothing more, nothing less. Let me tell you something. The day I find the woman of my dreams, everyone will know about it."

Ridiculous as it was, those words caused some of the tension to leave Eli's body.

Their mom turned to Roce. "What day will that be, my second born? How many more years do I have to live before that happens?"

"I'm not ready to settle down yet. You know that." He gave her a hug.

"You're impossible," she muttered. But she said it on a burst of laughter.

The need to escape drove Eli out of the room. "Solana's watching Libby tonight," he called over his shoulder. "I'll be back in the morning."

By the time he reached his truck, he was out of breath. He pressed his forehead against the steering wheel. Seeing Brianna Frost at the rodeo in her white cowboy hat convinced him he hadn't imagined his attraction to her at the gem shop.

Damn, was he ever glad she wasn't Roce's girlfriend.

MONDAY NIGHT, BRIANNA drove to the gem shop with her uncle. Her aunt thought they'd gone grocery shopping. They'd have to pick up a few items on their way home so she wouldn't get suspicious upon their return.

Mrs. Clayton greeted them when they walked into the warm, brightly lit store. But the first thing Brianna saw was little blue-eyed Libby with her floppy brunette curls, toddling around in front of the counter with her helicopter push toy. She was dressed in pink camo Wrangler jeans and a white-and-pink top with a ruffled hem. With Libby's matching pink cowboy boots, Brianna thought she'd never seen such an adorable child in her life!

"Hi, Libby."

The toddler recognized Brianna and pushed her toy toward her. Brianna got down on her haunches to examine her outfit. "Don't you look good enough to eat. Uncle Clark? This is Libby Clayton, Eli Clayton's daughter."

He tousled her curls. "She's a picture all right."

When he reached the counter Brianna heard him say, "Alberta? What a blessing to have such a beautiful granddaughter."

"Don't I know it!"

Brianna encouraged Libby to push her toy around. After a minute of doing an excellent job, Libby dropped it and held up her arms. "You want me to hold you? Oh, you little darling." She scooped her up and walked over to the counter with her.

Her uncle was examining the 1.5-carat pink sapphire solitaire. The way his eyes glowed as he looked at it told Brianna she'd chosen a winner. "I've never seen such a brilliant stone. I didn't know a pink sapphire could be such a deep color. Joanne will love it."

"It's definitely an eye-catcher. Which setting would you like?" Mrs. Clayton had put half a dozen rings on the velvet. He studied them.

"Which ring do you like, honey?"

"I like the white gold, but don't let what I think influence you."

"I think that would be my choice, too," the older woman concurred.

"Then let's do it, Alberta."

"Give me Joanne's size and I'll go in the back. It will only take me a few minutes to mount the stone. While you're here, maybe you'd like to look at some other stones."

She put out a display of sapphires sorted by col-

ors in trays that looked like cupcake tins. The natural
stones mined from the Sapphire Mountains came in
every color. When they were heated, their colors grew
more intense. Some were already a deep hue, but
those like the one Brianna had picked out were rare.

While her uncle stood looking at the sapphires,
Brianna walked around the shop with Libby, who
was back to pushing her toy. Each time the propeller
spun, the little girl laughed. "You must love to come
up here with your grandmother. It's fun, isn't it?"

Two hands patted Brianna's cheeks. Libby had an
endearing way. Brianna couldn't help kissing her.
"I love those little cowboy boots on your top." She
touched each one, causing the girl to giggle. In the
midst of it, Libby called out, "Dada!"

Brianna looked up, unaware that Eli Clayton had
entered the shop. Her pulse started to race. In a sheepskin jacket and boots, he looked the spitting image of
the tough, quintessential cowboy.

He's married, remember?

"It's Brianna, right?" His deep voice reverberated
through her body. She nodded. "I can see my daughter is very taken with you. She seems perfectly happy
to stay in your arms."

She had to admit she was surprised that Libby
hadn't reached for him yet. Did it upset him? Yesterday he'd been angry. Brianna moved closer to the
tall male to hand him his daughter, but Libby stayed
where she was. "I'm enamored with your little girl,"
she said. "She's too precious for words."

His eyes played over Brianna's features. "The feeling appears to be mutual. Come on, Libby. Time to go home for your dinner." He plucked her from Brianna's arms. His daughter made a sound of protest.

"You've got competition," his mother spoke up.

"You're right." He picked up the push toy and walked over to the counter to talk to Brianna's uncle. Libby clung to her daddy's shoulder, never taking her eyes off Brianna. The two men chatted briefly about Toly's performance at the rodeo.

"Sorry to barge in like this, Mom. I'll trade you this toy for her parka and we'll get going so you can get on with your business."

"We're finished," Mrs. Clayton said.

"I do believe my wife is going to be a happy woman." Uncle Clark smiled.

Mrs. Clayton handed Brianna's uncle the wrapped package. "I have no doubt of it."

"It's good to see you, Eli." He turned to Brianna. "Shall we go?"

"Yes. Don't forget we have to stop for some groceries on the way home." She waved to Libby. "Bye-bye, sweetie."

The little girl's lower lip wobbled and she started to cry. Uh-oh. Brianna's instinct to comfort her had to be squelched. She hurried out the door with her uncle behind her. They climbed into the truck and started heading down the mountain.

"It's a damn shame about Eli," her uncle muttered.

At the mention of his name, Brianna's heart leaped to her throat. "What do you mean?"

"Of course you wouldn't know. His wife had a

nervous breakdown after their baby was born. Roce said it was brought on by severe postpartum depression. She just couldn't get over it. It got to the point where Eli was playing both father and mother. His wife went back to her parents in Thompson Falls. She was too sick to handle being a mom and filed for a divorce Eli never wanted."

The air froze in Brianna's lungs. That explained the wedding band he still wore on his ring finger. He obviously still loved her and held out hope she'd recover so they could get back together. "How awful. That sweet little thing without her mommy."

"Life can throw you for a loop sometimes. Your aunt and I would have given anything to have a baby. The first time we tried to adopt, it fell through right at the end. On our second try, the birth mother lost the baby at seven months. Joanne couldn't bear the thought of another setback so we didn't try again."

"I'm so sorry."

He reached over and patted her arm. "We've been lucky your parents were willing to share you with us once in a while."

Too many emotions converged at once and tears trickled down Brianna's cheeks. "I'm the lucky one," she said.

Since his mother was ready to go home, Eli walked her out to the Land Rover. After giving Libby a kiss, she got in behind the wheel but didn't pull the door closed. Instead she stared hard at him the way only a mother could do.

"You've acted strangely the last two times you've come to the shop for Libby. The first night I saw a rudeness in you I didn't recognize. At the rodeo you didn't say two words. Tonight it was all you could do to be civil. I'm worried about you. What's going on? Don't tell me it's nothing."

Eli drew in a deep breath. "It's killing me that you're having to sacrifice so much for me. Before the week is out I'll contact an agency to help me find someone to watch Libby during the day. It won't be much longer before you have your freedom back."

"Libby is a joy! I don't ever want to hear you say that again, but I don't believe that's the reason for your behavior."

He held his daughter tighter. "I'm not sure I understand it myself."

Another silence followed. "Don't you think it's time you figured it out?" Streams of unspoken words flowed between them. "It's cold out here," his mother finally said. "Get Libby home and I'll see you two at breakfast."

Eli shut her door before getting in the truck with Libby. Once he'd fastened her in, they started down the snow-covered mountain. He passed Wymon's house and then Luis and Solana's. Eli's small ranch-style three-bedroom house sat closest to the main ranch house, two minutes away on foot.

After getting his daughter fed and bathed, he held her while they read her favorite story, *Goodnight Moon.* That was the book she always wanted him to read to her. Eli said the words over and over, hoping she'd repeat them. She fell asleep in his arms and he put her down in her crib.

Except for her hair color and eyes, his little girl resembled Tessa more than she resembled him. Eli had put photos of his ex-wife around the room so Libby would grow up knowing her. He leaned over the bars to watch her for a minute. A week after her birth, the nightmare had begun. Since then he'd experienced every range of human emotion while he grieved the breakup of his marriage. It had meant Libby had lost her mother.

For so long he'd been living in denial about everything. But tonight his mother's question about his state of mind had brought him up short. *Don't you think you'd better figure it out?*

The first sight of Libby so happy in Brianna Frost's arms had acted like a catalyst, jolting him out of the limbo in which he'd been wallowing. The anger he'd felt because it should have been Tessa holding their daughter had made him see red.

Worse, throughout this pain-filled year, he'd been blind to women. But, out of the blue, he'd found himself eating up Brianna Frost with his eyes when he knew his brother had brought her to the gem shop. Something earthshaking had happened to him over the last three days.

He left the nursery and walked across the hall to his bedroom. Deciding to take his mother's advice, he sat on the side of the bed and called his in-laws in Thompson Falls. It was the same time there. Quarter to nine.

They'd remained friends through all the grief and had stayed in touch. Diane and Carl Marcroft had driven down to Stevensville dozens of times in the past year to see their granddaughter. The divorce had been the last thing they'd wanted, but naturally they had to give Tessa their full support.

"Eli—" Diane had picked up on the second ring.

"Is this a bad time to call?"

"No. Tessa's downstairs in the TV room with Carl."

His hand tightened on the phone. "How is she?"

After a silence, "There's no improvement. Dr. Rutherford in Missoula has her on a new medication, but he thinks her condition may be chronic."

So nothing had really changed. That was the news Eli had needed to hear tonight in order to see things clearly.

"How's our Libby?"

"Growing cuter every day. Before bed tonight I took a picture of her in that pink outfit you sent her for Christmas. It should be on your phone."

"Oh, wonderful. I'll check it in a few minutes. How's Alberta?"

"Mom's just been terrific, as always."

"She's amazing. We feel so guilty for not being able to help more, but—"

"Don't go there," he broke in. "Tessa needs you full-time."

"What about you? We admire you so much, Eli."

"Thank you. To be honest, things are looking up. I've been saving money and am now able to pay for someone to watch Libby during the day. Hopefully by next week Mom will be able to get on with her own life."

"That's very good news, for both your sakes. We'll try to help all we can."

"You already do. Give my best to Carl. I'll call you again soon."

"We love you, Eli."

"Same here. Good night."

Eli clicked off. Diane didn't know it, but this call had given him the push to let go of the past and move in a new direction. No more hoping for something that wasn't going to happen. He looked down at his wedding ring. *Time to take this off for good, Eli.*

After removing it, he walked over to the dresser, where he put it and the picture he'd displayed of Tessa in the bottom drawer. He stared at the white skin where the ring had been. In the last year he'd experienced his father's death and the death of his own marriage. He'd suffered enough pain to last a lifetime. No more.

Before getting ready for bed, he phoned Luis and arranged to take Wednesday off work to check out employment agencies in Stevensville and Missoula. By next week he hoped to find a satisfactory nanny who could come to his house every Monday morning and leave after he got home from work every Friday evening.

The woman would need to have a car and could make the spare bedroom her own. She'd share the guest bathroom with Libby. He would expect her to prepare meals and do some light housekeeping. Her age didn't matter to him as long as she was the right fit for Libby.

As he climbed under the covers, the vision of his daughter patting Brianna Frost's cheeks replayed itself in his mind. Disturbed that he couldn't turn it off, he punched the pillow to get comfortable before oblivion took over.

THE JUSTIN BOOTS supplier came on Wednesday afternoons. Brianna opened the rear door of the saddlery to let him in while her uncle was out front dealing with a customer looking for the right saddle.

"How are you, Antonio?"

"Things are good, senorita, but they'd be better if you'd agree to go out with me tonight."

The rodeo celebrity from twenty years ago was probably in his midforties. According to her uncle, he'd been married and divorced twice. He had a certain reputation with the ladies. Brianna imagined he had several children with different women.

He lifted the last box off the dolly and put it on the floor. "What's it going to take?"

His bold approach and persistence annoyed her. "I've got a boyfriend," she lied.

"But you're not married yet."

All women were fair game to him. "That's true, but I'd like to be." Brianna counted the delivered inventory and signed the paper on his clipboard. "Accepting a date with another man would spell the end of my dreams, so I'm not taking any chances. Do you have any other business? My uncle's out front if you want to talk to him." She handed him the clipboard.

"No other business, *chica*."

Good. She'd angered him. Without wasting another minute, she walked over to the back door and opened it. "See you next week."

He pushed the dolly out the door. "*Hasta la vista*."

She shut the self-locking door and got busy unpacking boots and other items of clothing. Her uncle was whistling when she went out front with the delivered items. "I take it you made a sale."

"That's the third Dakota saddle this week. I'll have to place more orders."

"Your business is booming."

A smile broke out on his face. "We keep getting repeat customers. You're part of the reason."

"Nice one, Uncle Clark. You know I'm indebted to you."

"That works both ways. Your aunt can teach school without worrying about me running the saddlery alone. But any time you're ready to use that college degree to start a real career, you need only say the word."

"I know, but I'm very happy working here with you. To be honest, it makes me feel closer to Dad."

Her uncle squeezed her shoulder. "Same here."

She checked her watch. Ten after four. "Since today is your wedding anniversary, why don't you leave now so you can get ready to sweep Aunt Joanne off her feet. What's your plan?"

"I'm going to surprise her and pick her up at

school. We'll drive to Missoula and grab some dinner and then go country dancing."

"Ooh, I'd love to see the look on her face when she sees that ring."

"I'm excited, too."

"Then go home. I'll close up and see you two in the morning at breakfast."

"Thanks, honey." He gave her a hug and left the store. She had two more customers before it was time to lock the front door and put the closed sign in the window. With that done, she started for the back room but paused when she heard a knock on the window.

Brianna whirled around and almost fainted when she saw Eli Clayton's tall form through the glass. "Will you let me in for a minute?" he called out to her.

She nodded but couldn't imagine why he was there. Her heartbeat pounded in her ears as she unlocked the door. He stepped inside, bringing the cold air with him.

"If you've come to see my uncle, he left early."

He removed his hat. "I came by to talk to you."

Brianna smoothed her palms against her denim-clad hips. "Why?"

"After the way I treated you, you've got every right to ask that question." Those piercing blue eyes stared into hers. He was building up to something. "I want to apologize for my rude behavior at the gem shop last Saturday. Don't bother to deny it," he said before she could make a sound.

"I won't."

"At least that's honest," he muttered. "Several reasons were driving me at the time, but nothing excuses the way I acted. If my daughter had been old enough to express an opinion, she would have asked, 'Why are you being so mean, Daddy?'"

Brianna couldn't help smiling. "I realized something was wrong, but you didn't have to come here to explain."

"I disagree. If we could start again, I'd like to make up for it by taking you to dinner this evening. If you have other plans, then how about tomorrow night?"

Her second invitation of the day.

She couldn't say yes to him either, but for an entirely different reason.

Eli might be divorced, but he was still in love with his ex-wife. That made him off-limits to her. There was no way she dared accept an invitation to get to know him better.

"I accept your apology, but dinner isn't necessary."

"Then I did more damage than I thought," he said, his voice husky.

She shook her head. "Don't be silly." She took the few steps needed to open the front door so he would leave. "My aunt and uncle said your father was a true gentleman. Your visit here to make things right means it runs in your family. Consider that achieving your objective and have a lovely evening with your daughter, Eli."

He shoved the cowboy hat on his head at an angle and moved toward her. Beneath the brim, his shadowed gaze studied her features. "We'll meet again soon. Good night, Brianna."

"Good night."

After locking the door, she rushed through the store to the back room, where she turned off all the lights except for the ones in the display windows. Her legs were still trembling when she got into her truck and headed home. On the way she stopped at a drive-through for some pizza and a soda.

Once she got back, she didn't go inside the house right away. Instead she ate in the truck and called her brother, hoping he was available to talk. Carol answered and told her he was out in one of the sheds, but she'd have him call her ASAP.

No sooner did Brianna go inside the house than her phone rang. Seeing the caller ID, she hurried into the study and sat down on the couch. "Doug?"

"Hi, Brianna. You kept your promise to call me this week. What's up?"

She loved her brother so much. "Can you talk?"

"That's what we're doing, aren't we?"

"You know what I mean."

"I have all the time in the world for you. Carol's fixing dinner. Go ahead and tell me what's on your mind."

Brianna bit her lip. "I may have made a mistake tonight, and now I don't know what to do."

"Do I dare assume this has to do with a man?"

Clever Doug. His instincts were razor-sharp. "Yes."

"I take it he's a good one."

"Yes, I know he is. He has the most adorable fourteen-month-old daughter."

"Is he single? A widower? Divorced? Wait—he's not married, is he?"

"Doug—"

He chuckled. "You've got to give me more than a couple of yesses."

"I'm sorry. Let me ask you a hypothetical question. If you lost Carol—Heaven forbid if you did—how long do you think you'd stay in love with her?"

"I would always love her, but I don't think you can stay 'in love' forever because life has a way of evolving. I take it you've met a widower."

She breathed in deeply. "No. His ex-wife is alive, but he still wears his wedding ring."

"Yeah?" This after a brief silence. "That's a tricky one." It was not the response she'd been hoping for. "What mistake have you made, aside from falling for him?"

"I haven't fallen for him!"

"Then why ask me for advice?"

Brianna jumped up from the couch. "I barely know him, but I—I find him very attractive," she stammered. "That's all."

"Don't forget the adorable daughter."

That wasn't possible. Libby had his eyes.

"I don't want to be attracted to him."

Hearty laughter poured out of him. "Poor Brianna. After all those years of tying guys up in knots without compunction, you've found one who has turned the tables on you. What do you know…"

"Please don't make me feel worse."

"Now that I know a little more about the situation, how about telling me the nature of your second mistake?"

There was no getting around this with Doug, not when she'd phoned him. "He came to the saddlery a little while ago to apologize to me for something and asked me out to dinner. I told him I forgave him but that dinner wasn't necessary. Then I opened the door so he'd leave."

"And *did* he?"

"Yes."

"Good for him."

She winced.

"Why don't you tell me what happened for him to come to the store wanting to tell you he was sorry?"

"It's complicated."

"With you it usually is. Go on."

She told him everything that had gone on since the night Eli had been so rude at the gem shop. Quiet reigned after she'd finished explaining. "Doug?"

"You're frightened. Can't say I blame you, but he could still be wearing his wedding ring for a variety of reasons. At this early stage there's only one question you have to ask yourself. Is he so important to you that you won't be able to eat or sleep until you talk to him again and find out what's going on with him? In a few days you'll know if you can't get him off your mind."

"I'm afraid I already know." Her brother was right. "Thanks for listening to me."

"Anytime. Call me soon, okay?"

"I promise."

"Don't make promises you can't keep."

She chuckled. "Love you."

"Love you, too."

She hung up, hugging her arms to her chest. Yes, she was afraid. Eli had loved another woman, married her, had a baby with her. How did you compete with those memories? Did Brianna even want to try if it turned out he was interested in her?

Haunted by too many unanswerable questions, she went to her room and watched TV. Why did she have to meet a man who'd been married and had a past? A man who was still living in that past. A man with a darling little girl, who would remind him of his ex-wife every minute of their lives.

Brianna had no idea how long she stayed awake, tormented. It was a miracle that she finally slept. But when she awakened, she discovered her pillow drenched in tears.

Chapter Three

Eli cut a banana into pieces and put them on the tray of Libby's high chair. He ate one and then she ate one. Everything was a game with her.

"Mom? Are you sure you don't mind the applicants coming here this morning? I want to get your opinion before I take them up to my house." He'd narrowed the list down to three women. They'd be arriving in hourly intervals. The first one would be there in a few minutes.

"It's important we all meet, honey, and that includes Solana." The two of them sat at the kitchen table of the ranch house, enjoying coffee with their pancakes. Wymon had already left to meet up with Luis and the stockmen.

With Toly on the rodeo circuit and Roce in Missoula, Wymon needed Eli's help, but he'd taken this Wednesday morning off to conduct the nanny interviews. Life was about to change around here.

His mother eyed him with concern. "What's wrong?"

"Maybe none of them will be right and Libby won't like any of them."

"If things don't work out today, we can always interview more applicants." She eyed him over the rim of her coffee cup. "I didn't realize you'd removed your wedding ring. When did that happen?"

"Last week, after you advised me to get my act together. I phoned Tessa's family and had a talk with Diane. Nothing's changed with Tessa. The psychiatrist believes she might have chronic depression. I'd hoped in vain that she'd get better and want to come home." He shook his head. "It isn't going to happen, so I took the ring off and started looking for a nanny."

"You're very courageous. I'm proud of you, son."

"And I'm more grateful to you than you'll ever know for helping Libby and me through this last year."

He didn't hear his mother's response because Solana came into the kitchen. "Your first appointment has arrived. I showed her into the living room."

"Thanks, Solana." Eli got up from the chair. "Be right back." He tousled Libby's hair and headed for the other part of the house with little expectation that this could actually work.

By noon he'd found Sarah Giles, a cute young woman with an appealing personality whom everyone agreed would be great. Most important of all, Libby didn't cry when she picked her up and played with her.

She was twenty-eight and was living in Missoula with her grandparents while her husband was deployed with the army for the next fifteen months. They were saving their money and hoped to buy a house after his tour of duty was over.

Sarah had been trained as a cook and had worked as a sous-chef until recently. Cooking was her passion, but the restaurant had closed and she needed a job.

Eli decided that fifteen months with a nanny who could cook and keep his daughter happy sounded perfect. Sarah was ready to move in and would start work the next morning.

He was so relieved that he no longer had to rely on his mother for everything that he raced his horse Domino to the pasture. After telling Wymon his news, he did the job of three stockmen. They looked at him as if he'd lost his mind.

In a way, he had. Freed from a great source of worry for the first time in a year, he could concentrate on a plan to approach Brianna Frost again.

He'd never been shown the door before and was still smarting from the experience. In order to break through the barrier he'd caused her to erect, he needed backup. If anyone knew the way to Brianna's heart, Libby did.

When Saturday came around, he'd load his daughter in the truck just before closing time at the saddlery. On the pretext of wanting to buy her a child's cowboy hat, he'd ask Brianna for help. If he knew his little girl, she'd love the attention and wouldn't want to leave the shop. She might even start to cry, which would be a plus.

Eli would take it from there and suggest the three of them go for a bite to eat at a place where he could take Libby. A new sense of excitement filled him on his way back to the barn at dark. Tomorrow would be a new day and he had a good feeling about Sarah.

The last time Eli could remember looking forward to the future had been the night of Libby's birth. He'd felt such wonder as he held her in his arms. They'd started their family. At the time he couldn't have comprehended that they wouldn't live out a rich, full life together with more children.

The onset of Tessa's depression followed a week later and never went away. Eli had never suffered from chemical depression. But to watch it take hold of his wife and change her into someone he didn't know had devastated him. He'd been helpless to alleviate it or bring her comfort. She didn't want to hold Libby, let alone take care of her.

His whole family had pitched in to help and had been doing it ever since. Though Tessa's parents tried to do it long-distance, it was difficult.

On the night Tessa begged to go home, she didn't say, "I need to go back to my parents in Thompson Falls for a while." She'd made it clear she wanted to go *home*. That deliberate choice of words cut him to the quick and spelled the end of his dreams.

At the lowest point of his life, Eli packed up her things. After asking his mother to watch the baby, he drove Tessa back to her parents' house. The phone call asking for a divorce soon followed. What he'd feared most had come to pass, but the fact that it came as another shock proved to him he'd been living in denial.

He'd still been in denial until the day he'd seen Libby so happy in Brianna Frost's arms and realized he couldn't go on as he had been any longer. His mother's warning had acted as the catalyst for things to change, and he couldn't be more glad of the fact.

BRIANNA MET LINDSAY at the entrance to the Italian restaurant. "I'm glad you could meet me here for dinner. Ken works the night shift in the ER on Saturdays and I didn't want to go home to an empty house after work."

"I hear you. My aunt and uncle have gone to their monthly Cattlemen's Association dinner. This was a great idea."

They went inside. Naturally the restaurant was crowded, being as it was a weekend night. The hostess showed them a table and handed them menus. Brianna opened hers. "So what do you think you're in the mood for?"

Her friend looked over her own menu. "I think I'll order the alfredo with mushrooms."

"Mmm, that sounds good, but so does the chicken Tuscany."

"Let's get both and share. Now that I'm over my morning sickness, I eat like a horse."

Brianna chuckled. "Perfect."

They gave the waitress their order. "That book on Elon Musk you were asking about came in. I'll save you a copy if you want."

"I'll come by Monday on my lunch hour to buy it."

"Why don't you just buy a Kindle?"

"I could, but I like a book in my hands, you know?"

"I do, too."

They were still talking books when the waitress brought their meal. Lindsay's eyes lit up. "Wow, this looks good."

"It does. I'm starving."

Halfway through their meal Lindsay leaned forward. "Don't make it too obvious, but you've got to get a look at this cowboy who just walked in carrying an adorable little girl wearing a cowgirl hat," she whispered. "If I weren't married…"

Brianna tried to turn her head inconspicuously and almost slid off her chair. Catching her breath, she faced her friend once more. "Even if you were single, you wouldn't want to get involved with him."

Lindsay blinked. "You know him?"

"I've met him several times. His name is Eli. He's one of the Clayton brothers."

Her friend sat back in surprise. "You're talking *Toly* Clayton's brother?"

"That's right."

"Wow."

"My uncle told me Eli's wife divorced him. But he still wears his wedding ring."

"He probably does that to keep all the women away. Otherwise there'd be a line a mile long."

A piece of chicken lodged in Brianna's throat. She had to take a drink of water to clear it. "I was thinking he can't take it off because he's still so much in love with her."

Lindsay went quiet. Brianna found herself the object of her friend's gaze. "What aren't you telling me?"

"It doesn't matter."

"I think it does," Lindsay said right back. "You're interested in him."

"Well, like you, I find him attractive."

"And?"

She averted her eyes. "And nothing."

"Has he asked you out?"

By now Brianna was squirming. "Yes, but I turned him down."

"Brianna—why?"

"I told you."

Lindsay kept at her. "Is it because he has a daughter?"

"No! She's wonderful."

"So you've met her, too." Her friend smiled. "If you want my advice, which I know you don't, I would tell him yes if you get another chance."

"That's not going to happen."

"Don't be so sure. He's walking this way."

What? Her heart thundered in her chest.

"Brianna?"

She looked up and her gaze collided with Eli's. At the same moment his daughter tried to get to her. Brianna pushed her chair back. "Hi, Libby. Have you come out to dinner with your daddy?"

By now the little girl was twisting to escape Eli's

arms. Brianna had no choice but to reach for her. His little girl wrapped her arms around Brianna's neck, warming her heart.

Eli's blue eyes glittered with amusement. "When we came in for dinner, she spotted you out of all these people. Your hair is unmistakable. I gave up any hope of peace until we came over to say hi first."

"Why don't you join us?" Lindsay spoke up with a knowing smile Brianna had already deciphered. "We have two more chairs."

Brianna moaned inwardly.

"I don't want to intrude."

"It's no intrusion, is it, Brianna?"

"No, of course not. Please sit down."

"I'm Lindsay Turner, Brianna's friend," Lindsay said as he pulled out a chair. "And you are…"

"Eli Clayton."

"Well, Mr. Clayton, I have to say that's the cutest little girl I ever saw in my life, especially in that cowgirl hat. I'm expecting in four months and can't wait to start dressing my daughter."

"Congratulations. I'm happy for you. We bought this hat at the saddlery before coming here. She went right to the one she wanted and put it on her head. That was it."

He'd come by the store? Had her uncle told him she'd be at the restaurant?

"It's my favorite one," Brianna admitted. The white felt with the pink trim and star looked as if it had been designed for his daughter.

"But it needs to come off while we eat, or you

won't be able to finish your dinner." Brianna watched as Eli leaned over and undid the tie before lifting it off his daughter's head.

His ring.

It was gone!

Libby didn't seem to mind being relieved of her hat, but Brianna sat there in shock to see the white skin where the band had been. From Brianna's lap the little brown-haired princess wanted to touch everything and reached for Brianna's roll. She darted Eli a glance. "Is it all right?"

"If it is with you. She eats everything. I'll order you another one with her mac and cheese." He signaled the waitress to come over and asked for a high chair.

While Brianna fed Libby a spoonful of linguine from her plate, Eli and Lindsay discussed Toly's recent wins. Soon Eli's order arrived, but, to Brianna's consternation, Lindsay had finished her meal and stood up.

She smiled at Brianna. "If you'll excuse me, I'm going to take what I didn't finish to my husband while it's still kind of warm. I promised him." Brianna had feared this would happen. "Thanks for having dinner with me. I'll see you on Monday at noon."

"I'll be there."

Eli got to his feet. "It was nice to meet you."

"I'm so glad to have met you and your daughter, Mr. Clayton. Wait till I tell my husband that I had dinner with Toly Clayton's brother. We're both great fans."

"I'll tell him," Eli said and smiled.

After she walked away, Eli plucked his daughter from Brianna's lap and put her in the high chair. He set it right next to Brianna so Libby wouldn't complain and started feeding her macaroni while he ate his spaghetti and meat balls.

He eyed her. "Would you believe I had intended to ask you to have dinner with me and Libby tonight at this same restaurant? I was disappointed you'd left the saddlery early so I didn't get the chance to ask. Seeing you here was fortunate for us, but I didn't mean to break up your plans for the evening."

She sat back in the chair. "Please don't worry about it. Lindsay works at the bookstore in the mall and we eat lunch together a lot. She was just anxious to take her husband, Kenneth, a treat. He's a doctor doing his internship in emergency medicine at the hospital and has been working a lot of nights lately."

"Lucky man to have such a devoted wife."

Brianna nodded. "They're a great couple."

"A baby will change their lives," Eli said. A wealth of emotion lay behind his words. "Libby sure has changed mine."

"I can only imagine."

"As you've learned, my mother has been watching her since the divorce. But a few days ago I hired a nanny so I can get on with my ranching duties. She seems to be working out well." He drank part of his coffee. "Speaking of the ranch, did your aunt like the ring you purchased from the gem shop?"

"She loves it. My uncle is definitely in her good books after that gift."

A smile broke the corner of his mouth. "Maybe I should give you a sapphire so I can get in yours."

Heat filled her cheeks. "I'm sorry if I gave you the wrong impression."

"You had every right to turn me down, but I still have a problem because I would like to get to know you better. Are you dating someone?"

She could lie about it, but she didn't want to because he was a good man who deserved the truth. "Not right now."

"So it *was* my bad manners that ruined my chances."

If he only knew the truth...

"Since my nanny is willing to do some babysitting at night if I want to go out, I'm going to try this once more. Will you have dinner with me next Tuesday? If the answer is no, then I'll never bother you again."

The finality of that remark drove her to a quick response. She had to take that chance, even though it scared the living daylights out of her. "Sure," she said. "I'll have dinner with you next Tuesday."

A look of satisfaction entered his eyes. "Good. I'll pick you up at your uncle's house. I thought we'd go to Chez Maurice, the new French restaurant. Shall we say seven o'clock?"

"That will give me time to leave work and get ready." Brianna hadn't been to that restaurant yet, but she'd heard it was pretty fancy. On that note, she reached for her purse and got up from the table. When he made a motion to stand, she said, "Please, Eli, stay where you are so it won't upset your daughter. I'm just going to slip away. Enjoy your dinner and I'll see you on Tuesday."

Before Libby realized what was happening, Brianna hurried over to the counter to pay her bill and left the restaurant for home. She felt shaky—and more excited than the situation warranted. Libby had provided a buffer tonight, but the next time she saw him, he'd be without her. The thought made her nervous.

Don't forget, Brianna. Just because he's removed his wedding ring doesn't mean his heart has stopped longing for the woman he married.

A HUGE WINTER storm front moved in Monday night. On Tuesday Eli and Wymon spent the day with the stockmen, rounding up strays and making certain the cattle had enough food. They talked about the lawsuit against the Bureau of Land Management that their father had taken out while he was still alive because they'd been charged taxes for the acid mine drainage coming out of their mine.

They had little time left to clean up before a larger tax would be levied against them. A good chunk of their ranch money was tied up because of it, something that worried the whole family. Eli didn't get back to the house until ten after six and had to rush to get ready for his evening with Brianna.

Libby didn't like being denied the usual time he spent with her. He didn't like it either and could hear her fussing as he walked out the door. But Sarah would cheer her up. She had a great way of handling his daughter. He left the house, knowing Libby was in good hands, and headed for the Frost home.

It was hard to believe he was going on his first date with a woman in years. He'd thought he'd put all that behind him when he'd married Tessa. Some of the divorced guys he knew said that dating again was just like riding a bike. Once you got on, it all came back to you. The hell it did. He was nervous, an emotion he'd never experienced around women in his life.

When he pulled into the shoveled driveway, Clark Frost was just putting his snowblower away in the garage. The two men greeted each other before Eli went to the front door and rang the bell. A German shorthair squeezed into the opening first.

Brianna looked like a vision in a belted, camel-hair wool coat that ended above the knee. In the hall light her collar-length blond hair took on an ethereal quality. The creamy pink lipstick drew his attention to round, full lips.

"You made it here." She sounded slightly breath-less.

"I haven't yet met a storm I couldn't handle."

She laughed. "Good night, Taffy," she said, patting the dog's head. "See you later." The shorthair's low moan sounded as she closed the door.

Eli cupped her elbow and walked her to his truck. The small, gold side buckles on her black high-heeled ankle boots completed her classy outfit. He couldn't take his eyes off her. A flowery fragrance wafted past him as he helped her into the cab, nearly undoing him.

Most of the streets had been plowed. They drove across town to Chez Maurice and discussed what their day had been like. She cast him a sideward glance. "How did Libby handle you leaving her?"

"She made sounds like your dog."

"It's no fun being left behind."

"You should have heard her after you walked out of the restaurant Saturday night. I'm convinced people thought I was a child beater. Any thought of a fun evening with my daughter went up in flames."

"I'm sure you're exaggerating."

"Maybe a little, but clearly she didn't want you to leave. Luckily, the nanny's working out well, so my mother can lead her own life again."

"Tell me about your nanny."

"Sarah Giles is married," he started by saying. He filled her in on the woman's background. "She's good with Libby. When her husband gets back from his deployment I'll have to find another nanny, but for now I'm really happy."

"If Libby likes her, that's all that really matters."

He pulled into the plowed parking lot and walked her inside. The maître d' led them to a candlelit table for two by the fireplace. After the freezing cold outside, he felt Brianna breathe in its warmth with pleasure.

The simple act of removing her coat caught him off guard. He wanted to pull her against him and knew he was already in trouble. There was nothing like firelight. The glow outlined her feminine figure dressed in a simple knee-length black dress with cap sleeves.

They sat across from each other. "I took the liberty of ordering our dinner ahead of time." He poured the white wine brought to their table and lifted his glass. "To you, Brianna. I haven't been on a date with another woman in almost three years."

She took a sip. "How did you meet your wife? I hope you don't mind my asking."

"Not at all. We met at college in Missoula."

"Was it love at first sight?"

"No. We grew on each other after studying together. Pretty soon we were spending so much time together that we decided to get married. Her breakdown after the baby made me realize we don't always know everything about each other, even if we think we do."

"I'm sorry, Eli."

"It's life." He took a swallow. "Now it's your turn to reveal the unadorned truth about yourself."

Her features sobered. "Unadorned, huh? Hmm. Well, I was proposed to twice, but I didn't get married because I never met the right man for me." She finished her wine and put the glass down.

"How old are you?"

"I'll be twenty-four on February 14."

"A *Valentine* baby." Amazing.

"It's the best birthday on earth. Everyone remembers it and I'm given so much chocolate I have to go on a diet for a month."

He loved it. "I've never known anyone born on that day before."

"I know of three: Jimmy Hoffa, Jack Benny and Carl Bernstein."

He chuckled. Her personality was growing on him like mad.

"How old are you, Eli?"

"I'll be twenty-seven on the Fourth of July."

"You're kidding!"

"Nope! Same birthday as Calvin Coolidge."

A smile lit up her lovely face. "That has to be the birthday of all birthdays."

He grinned. "It probably comes close to yours."

Brianna laughed gently before the waiter brought their chateaubriand to the table. Once he had left, they were alone once more and began to eat. "This is delicious, Eli. To get good French food back home, we used to drive to the Napa Valley, but it was a hundred miles away."

"Who is 'we'?"

"My parents and brother. Now that my parents are gone, he and his wife live in our family home and run the fruit farm."

He studied her features. "I'm sure you miss them."

She nodded. "But they're newlyweds and deserve some time to themselves."

The answer to his next question was of vital importance to him. "How long are you going to stay with your aunt and uncle?"

"I'm not sure. I graduated from college with a business degree right before my parents were killed. My aunt and uncle saved my life by asking me to come and live with them for a while. One of these days

I'll get my act together and do something with my degree. But to tell you the truth, I like my job at the saddlery. Uncle Clark is so much like my dad that it helps lessen the pain just being around him."

"I can relate. My brothers are made up of parts of my father. Family means everything." While they talked about their families, the waiter brought them their dessert.

As soon as she saw the chocolate mousse, she flashed him a wide, natural smile that lit up his universe. "How did you know I love chocolate?"

"The truth is I guessed. Who doesn't love chocolate?"

Between the wine and the warmth of the fire, he felt pleasantly relaxed for the first time in ages. He could tell she'd been affected, too. Her eyelids fluttered and there was a pretty flush on her cheeks. If they were alone at his house, he wouldn't let her leave. How unfortunate that all good things had to come to an end and he would have to take her home soon.

"Eli Clayton—it *is* you!" declared a male voice from the past, snapping him out of his endorphin-induced haze.

Chapter Four

Eli turned his head. "Don—" He got to his feet. "How are you?" They shook hands. "It's been a long time."

"You can say that again."

"Haven't you been working in Missoula all this time?"

"That's over since I've just been promoted to bank manager here."

"Congratulations."

"Thanks. You're still ranching, I presume?"

"Always," Eli muttered. He was acutely aware of the way Don kept staring at Brianna. His old nemesis was still single and it showed.

"I heard Tessa divorced you and went back to Thompson Falls." Don never did understand boundaries or show sensitivity. "I take it the baby is with her?"

"No. Libby lives with me."

Don rocked on his heels. "I didn't realize. Who's this heavenly creature?" he asked, speaking directly to Brianna.

"A friend."

"You're not on the rodeo circuit anymore, yet you still manage to find the hotties, eh?"

Eli bristled.

"Aren't you going to introduce us?"

"Sure." He darted a glance at her. "Brianna Frost, meet Don Shapiro. He's the new manager of the Bitterroot-Sapphire Bank Branch here in Stevensville."

She nodded. "How do you do?"

"It's my pleasure. Frost? That name is familiar, but you're not from Stevensville or I would have remembered you. I was born here and went all through school with the Clayton boys."

"I see. I'm from Marysville, California. I'm just living with my aunt and uncle for a while."

"Now I remember. Clark Frost. He does business at the bank and owns the saddlery. Is he your uncle?"

"Yes. I work at the saddlery."

"Well, what do you know. I'll have to drop by."

Eli had taken all he could and put some bills on the table. "If you'll excuse us, Don, we were on the verge of leaving. Ready, Brianna?" He walked around and held her coat whether she wanted to leave or not. She stood up so he could help her put it on.

"I was going to ask you to join me and my friends at our table."

"Another time maybe. Thanks anyway. I imagine I'll see you again." *But not if I can help it.*

They said good-bye and he ushered Brianna out of the restaurant into the frigid night air. After the contentment he'd felt being with her, the unwelcome intrusion had turned their dinner into something else, leaving a bitter taste in his mouth. In the foulest of moods, he drove them back to her family's home.

"I take it he wasn't a close friend."

His hand tightened on the steering wheel. "What an irony. Tonight I wanted to explain the reasons why I was so rude when we first met. Now I find myself needing to apologize again. I'm afraid I'm not fit company, Brianna. Your instincts were right the first time." He pulled into the driveway but kept the engine running so they'd stay warm.

"If it will make you feel any better, he reminded me of Antonio Perez, the salesman who comes around the saddlery every once in a while and annoys the heck out of me. I was glad we left when we did. Somehow I can't see him as the manager of a bank. The poor tellers. Was the transfer a demotion, do you think?"

Eli threw his head back and laughed. "He'd be crushed to hear you say that. The dude couldn't take his eyes off you, but I suspect that happens to you on a regular basis."

"Of course it doesn't. If I may be so bold, what is the history between you two?"

"He comes from a prominent local ranching family, but he couldn't cut it on the rodeo circuit."

"Ah—" she exclaimed. "According to Uncle Clark, the Clayton boys are rodeo legends in Montana. He told me you were a champion bull rider like your dad."

"I was average. Toly's the best bull rider of all of us."

"Well, if Mr. Shapiro wanted to compete and couldn't make the grade, then that had to be tough on him. But mentioning your wife and daughter in front of me was rude. I thought you handled the situation well. If I'd been you, I would probably have knocked his block off."

The woman sitting next to him had a way about her that calmed the beast in him. "Thanks for your understanding."

"Thank *you* for a lovely evening and delicious dinner. What I'm waiting for is the explanation you promised me about your feelings the first time we met."

Eli sucked in his breath. "You mean now? In the truck?"

"Why not. It's cozy and warm in here and no one will bother us."

He grinned. "I wouldn't count on that. If your uncle thinks I've been here long enough, I wager he'll make his presence known."

Her chuckle made its way inside him. "I can take care of him," she said, and he had no doubt of it. "Seriously, Eli, what happened? I didn't know Libby belonged to you when you first walked in, and I couldn't understand why you were upset simply because I was holding her for your mother."

"The night I entered the gem shop and saw Libby so happy in another woman's arms, it killed me that it wasn't Tessa holding her."

"Oh. That would have been painful."

"It was. At first I was in denial about the seriousness of Tessa's postpartum depression. We'd been so excited about the baby coming and had outfitted the nursery, but a week after the delivery she turned into a completely different person. Those dark days ran into a month. She lost interest in the baby, in me. That never changed."

"Oh, Eli. I'm so sorry."

"I was sorry, too, but mostly for our daughter, who wasn't able to bond with her mother. The psychiatrist said her depression was severe and she might never want to be with the baby. I was horrified. It was up to me, Mom and Solana to take care of Libby.

"Soon after, Tessa told me she wanted to go home to her parents. I had no choice but to drive her to Thompson Falls. Two weeks later I got a phone call from her asking for a divorce. I fought it in my heart."

"Of course," Brianna whispered. "I can't even imagine."

"I wanted us to be a family. Libby needed her, but all the wanting in the world didn't change anything. Her parents urged me to agree to it. They hoped it might help her to calm down. The psychiatrist thought it was for the best, too.

"So I signed the papers. She gave up all parental rights to Libby."

"Eli? Does it mean that if she got better and wanted to be a mother, she couldn't?"

"Legally, yes, but it's just a piece of paper. I'd give anything if she wanted to see Libby, and I would do anything to make it happen. Every child deserves his or her own mother."

"Who could blame you for wanting that?" A troubled sigh escaped her lips.

"I was a mental wreck that night at the gem shop. I'd stopped at the ranch house earlier. Solana told me my brother had brought a woman with him from Missoula and they'd gone up to the gem shop. There you were with Roce. My mind jumped to the wrong conclusion that you were his girlfriend."

"It's all making sense," she murmured.

"What I'm about to tell you will convince you to avoid me at all costs."

"Why don't you let me be the judge of that?"

"This last year I've been functioning in a dark cloud of pain and anger. When I saw you with Libby, several things struck me at once. You were beautiful and I found myself attracted to you, even though Roce had met you first. I was so disgusted with myself over my thoughts that I couldn't get out of the shop fast enough." He ran a hand over his face. "Now that you know the truth, I'll walk you to the house."

"Wait—" she said as he reached for the door handle.

"There isn't any more, Brianna."

"You've had your turn. Now I need time to explain my behavior to you."

"What do you mean?"

"When you apologized to me at the store and asked me to go to dinner, I turned you down. But it wasn't because I couldn't forgive your rudeness."

"Then I don't know what you're getting at."

"A man who asks out a single woman while still wearing his wedding ring sends her one clear message—he doesn't honor his marriage." When Eli started to say something, she put up her hands to stop him. "I know. At the time you'd wanted to apologize to me in the nicest way possible, but I couldn't risk it."

"I don't understand."

She lowered her head. "I'd had thoughts, too. Thoughts that disgusted me."

Intrigued, he leaned closer. "Why?"

She sighed. "You've been so honest that I have to do the same. The truth is that first time I saw you at the gem shop I felt an instant attraction to you, too, but you were a married man. There was a ring on your finger. At the time I didn't know you were divorced."

What? His heart started to thud.

"To get involved with a married man goes against my principles and I got angry because I hadn't been able to control my emotions. I asked myself why I didn't feel that way about Roce, who didn't wear a wedding band on *his* finger and who couldn't have been kinder to me."

Good grief. They'd both been so wrong about everything. "Did he ask you out?"

"No. But he said the next time he came through Stevensville, he'd drop by the saddlery and we'd go out for a meal."

Roce had been interested. Any red-blooded man would be.

"Before you jump to any more conclusions, I can

tell you now that he was only being nice to me. If he'd been serious, he would have asked for my phone number and made a definite date."

Eli sat back. "Do you still feel it's a risk to go out with me?"

"Yes. After what you've admitted to me tonight, I know it is."

He ground his teeth in reaction. "What exactly did I say?"

"I heard the intensity of your emotion when you said you'd give anything if your ex-wife wanted to see Libby. You said you'd do anything to make it happen. If ever a man sounded like he was still in love with his wife, you do."

"Brianna—"

"Let me finish. No woman would want to compete with the woman who holds your heart. Your Tessa might improve enough to want you and your daughter back. Anything is possible in this world. Miracles do happen. I will pray for you and Libby that it does."

She unexpectedly opened the door. "I loved this evening and the time spent so we could be honest with each other. One thing I've learned in the short time we've had together—you're a great father. I had a great one, too. Libby is luckier than she'll ever know. Don't give up on winning your wife back. The chemistry in the brain can change. Good-bye, Eli Clayton. You're the best."

He sat there in shock as she got out of the truck and hurried to the front door. When she let herself inside and turned off the porch light, he felt pain rip him apart as if a bull had stomped on his heart until it was a pulpy mess. Her admission that she'd been attracted to him, too, was negated when in the next breath she'd accused him of still being in love with Tessa.

Eli backed out of the driveway and headed home while the question over his feelings for his ex-wife forced him to dig deep in his soul. He would always love Tessa and the memory of her. But they hadn't lived as man and wife since the baby came. The flame that had kept their love alive had been smothered by illness.

Had it gone out completely? He would have to be with Tessa again to feel if there was any love coming from her before he could answer that question.

Once inside the house he walked to Libby's room and stood over her crib for a long time. His precious daughter lay flat on her back. Her favorite white polar bear was jammed against the top of her head. In her pink-and-white sleeper pajamas, she looked like a little angel with tangled brown curls who'd just popped out of Heaven.

His thoughts returned to Brianna and he lowered his forehead to the crib railing.

Brianna had said good-bye to him tonight and she'd meant it. He had no choice but to give her the space she wanted. But he didn't have to sit around and wonder what his heart was telling him about Tessa. Despite their divorce, he needed to see her a final time. It was vital he look in her eyes and talk about their daughter. Eli had stayed away from her more than long enough.

SATURDAY MORNING ELI stopped by the ranch house with Libby. "Mom?"

"Hi, honey. I'm in the kitchen." He walked through, carrying his daughter in his arms. "Oh, what a wonderful surprise!" She reached out to hug her. "What brings you here? I hope you're going to stay a while. I've missed you."

"We've missed you, too, but today we have plans. I'm going to be gone most of the day and wanted you to know why in case you tried to find me for some reason."

His mother gave him the discerning eye. "This sounds serious."

"It is. I'm leaving for Thompson Falls. I know Tessa and I are divorced, but I feel it's necessary that she sees us again. Perhaps nothing will ever change with her, but I'm giving it one last chance."

His mother waited a beat before she said, "You haven't put your ring back on."

"No. I want *that* plus the sight of Libby in my arms to be a surprise, along with my unexpected visit. I'm not the tormented, crushed man she remembers divorcing. Since she wouldn't have anything to do with Libby after being home a week, this will be my own version of shock therapy to find out if seeing her again changes anything. I owe it to our daughter to make this last attempt."

"And to you," his mother added. "Her parents don't know you're coming?"

He shook his head. That would take away the element of surprise, the one thing he was counting on.

She put a hand on his arm. "Tessa's a very lucky woman to have had such an honorable husband. Drive safely. Whatever happens, remember that you're doing a very unselfish thing today. When your daughter is older, she will bless you for trying."

Her comment let him know his mother didn't place a lot of faith in anything changing, but she still supported him. Eli's throat swelled with emotion. "Thanks, Mom. I love you."

He gave her a kiss and left the house for the truck. His little cherub sat in the back, strapped in her car seat. She had no clue where they were going and didn't care while she played with one of her doughnut toys.

Thompson Falls was located in a beautiful valley in northwest Montana along the Clark Fork River, two and a half hours from the ranch. He and Tessa had done a lot of fishing there with her parents.

The sun peeked in and out of the cloud cover all the way. Snow blanketed the familiar landscape, but he didn't feel the pain he'd felt the last time he'd made this journey without the baby.

His world was different now. He had a daughter who was growing up fast and needed all his love. There was also a blonde woman he wasn't ready to walk away from at this early stage, not by a long shot. Brianna's words continued to resound in his head. *Don't give up on winning your wife back.* It was good advice, if not for him, for Libby. But this would be his last attempt.

Eli sat back and turned on the radio to a soft rock

station. This was the longest trip he'd taken with Libby to date. Every so often, he stopped to change her diaper and give her snacks. He noticed she'd been sneezing. Maybe it was a winter allergy of some kind, but he didn't think a great deal about it.

In St. Regis he stopped for gas and bought a couple of Snickers bars for himself. Then, at ten after eleven, he pulled into the Marcrofts' driveway.

It was a Saturday, and Eli imagined Tessa's family would likely be at home with her. Their cars were probably in the garage. He got out and reached for his daughter, whom he'd dressed in the pink outfit they'd sent.

"This is it, sweetie. You're going to see your mother for the first time since you were a tiny newborn." Her answer was another sneeze.

"Hey, what's going on with you?" He kissed her cheeks and then approached the front door and rang the bell. After a minute it opened.

Tessa stood in the entrance, looking like a person who'd seen a ghost.

"Eli—" she gasped. "My parents aren't here."

Maybe that was just as well. She clung to the door. He had the feeling that she was ready to close it on him.

"Naturally, I would enjoy seeing them, but Libby and I came to visit you."

The last time they'd been together was when he'd driven Tessa to her parents' house for good. Since then she seemed to have lost about five pounds. He could tell because her jeans were loose on her. Otherwise she was the same woman who'd given birth to their little girl, who was a replica of her with that brown hair and heart-shaped face.

Tessa's features froze. "If you're here to tell me you want me back—"

Even though Tessa had spoken in a low voice, Libby hid her face in his neck like she did when confronted by a stranger. It brought out his protective instincts and he held her closer.

"Not at all," he interjected quietly. "I came to grips with our divorce quite a while ago." She couldn't help but see he'd removed his wedding ring.

"Then I wish you'd leave."

Eli saw no sign in her brown eyes that she'd missed him or thought about him. Was it the medication, or her depression, or both that produced that vacant stare?

He supposed he'd never know. A wealth of memories bombarded him, but oddly enough the only emotion he felt was one of sorrow for his daughter, who would never know her mother.

"I realize this has come as a complete surprise. I didn't let your parents know my plans, either, but I thought you might want to see Libby just this once."

He saw her flinch, whether in fear, regret, anger, resentment, he couldn't tell.

"Now that you've accomplished your goal, I'm going to shut the door."

"Before you do that, I just want to be sure you haven't changed your mind about giving up your rights to her. Though you signed them away, I would never keep her from you. Wouldn't you like to hold Libby for a moment?"

Eli waited for her to answer, hoping that her hesitation meant she was considering it.

She acted nervous. "I can't believe you had the nerve to come here like this unannounced and uninvited." Her voice faltered.

Eli took a deep breath. "It will never happen again. Good-bye, Tessa."

Turning on his heel, he walked toward the truck with his daughter's head bobbing against his shoulder. After strapping Libby in her car seat, he got behind the wheel and backed out of the driveway just as Tessa's parents were pulling in.

They got out of their car and hurried toward him. "Eli?" Carl spoke first while Diane opened the back door to give Libby a hug. His little girl sneezed again. "Bless you, darling. We didn't know you were coming."

"I meant it to be a surprise. I needed to be certain that, after seeing Libby this time, Tessa still felt the same about signing away her rights. She didn't show any interest at all."

Tessa's father shook his head sadly.

"I got my answer for myself, Carl, and promised she'd never see me again. I'll make that same promise to you. Please forgive me. I realize it was taking a risk to show up uninvited. No doubt she'll need to talk to her therapist about what happened today."

Diane came around to the driver's side of the truck. "There's nothing to forgive. I'm glad you forced her to face Libby. Tessa's therapist had suggested a visit before but Tessa was always so indifferent to the advice. Seeing her daughter again after all this time is something she has needed no matter how much she has pushed you away. We love our Libby and you."

"The feeling's mutual."

Carl patted Eli's shoulder through the window. "We'll drive to Stevensville soon to spend time with the two of you."

"We'd love that. You'd better go in to Tessa. Thanks for being so understanding."

After giving Libby more hugs and kisses, they stepped away from the truck and he drove down the street anxious to get back to the ranch. His little girl would need to run around and stretch her legs after another two-and-a-half-hour trip in the truck.

To his surprise her sneeze had turned into cough. She'd definitely picked up some kind of bug. When they arrived at the house, he'd take her temperature. If she got stuffed up, he'd put the old steamer in her room to ward off a full-fledged cold.

His mind relived today's visit. It had probably set Tessa back, but Eli wasn't sorry he'd made the trip. It amazed him what a year away from her had done to his feelings for her. She'd retreated to a place he couldn't go and wasn't welcome. He couldn't relate to the woman she'd become.

Eli had talked with Tessa's therapist at the beginning. The doctor had told him there were physical reasons behind postpartum depression that had to do with a change in hormones. Hers had turned out to be a severe case. More important, she'd become sleep deprived and anxious about her ability to care for the baby.

Add to that a feeling of being less attractive. The doctor suspected Tessa struggled with her sense of identity and the fact that she'd lost control over her life. Hearing that explanation, Eli had suffered greatly because of his feelings of hopelessness, but those days were over now.

He was glad that he'd taken Brianna's advice. Seeing his ex-wife today had not only proved to him that his heart was whole again, but he'd also accepted the truth. Tessa had left him and would never be coming back. From here on out he was going to make a brand-new life with his little girl and embrace it.

Once back at his house, he fixed dinner for Libby and himself. She wasn't very hungry and still had a cough but not a temperature. His mother came over and they played with his daughter until it was time to put her to bed. After setting up the steamer near the crib, they crept out of the nursery into the living room.

His mother darted a glance at him. "You seem good."

"I *feel* good. Diane said she was glad I forced Tessa to see Libby. When I drove away from the house, I knew in my gut it was the right thing to have done."

"I agree. What made you decide to do it?"

"It was something Brianna Frost said to me the other night after I took her out to dinner."

"What was that?"

"Don't give up on your wife. Then she said good-bye to me."

"As in—"

"Good-bye for real."

"I see. Does she know your history? That you're divorced?"

He nodded.

"That's interesting."

"Not really. She thinks I'm still in love with Tessa. Because I was wearing my wedding ring when we first met at the gem shop."

"That's right. You were."

"Yup, but she's wrong about my feelings. Tessa was my first love, but I've known for a long time that I'm no longer in love with her. I hated admitting to failure. That's why I kept wearing the ring. But to-day's visit helped me see that our marriage wasn't a failure. It just couldn't succeed. I drove away with the knowledge that it was truly over and it has steered me in a new direction. I feel so liberated."

"That's the best news I've heard in a very long time. Good night, honey. Don't forget Sunday din-ner tomorrow, but if Libby gets worse, call me if you need me, even if it's the middle of the night."

He walked her to the door. "You know I will. Thanks, Mom."

Eli gave her a hug and watched her walk out to the Land Rover. Tomorrow evening he had a phone call to make to Brianna and would be counting the hours until then. He expected pushback, but he wasn't going to let that stop him from being with her again. She'd lit a fire in him the first time he'd laid eyes on her. He knew himself too well. The flame was far too strong for anything to extinguish it now.

Chapter Five

Late Tuesday afternoon the saddlery phone rang while Brianna was finishing up with a customer. Her uncle had already gone home. She handed the rancher his box of new boots before picking up.

"Good afternoon. Frosts' Saddlery."

"Brianna Frost?" The male voice was familiar, but it wasn't her brother or Roce Clayton or Antonio Perez or Asa Harding, who worked on a nearby ranch. It certainly wasn't the cowboy she'd made certain she would never hear from again. Big mistake, as she'd found out after too many sleepless nights.

Her hand tightened on the receiver. She hated it when a caller started out by blurting her full name that way. It made her nervous. "May I help you?" she asked.

"I'm planning on it."

The man's arrogance rang a bell. Don Shapiro from the bank. "I'm sorry, but I don't know who this is," she lied.

"It's Don Shapiro."

"Oh, Mr. Shapiro. I'm afraid my uncle isn't here. If

this is urgent bank business, I can reach him at home and have him call you."

"Whoa, whoa, honey. I'm calling to ask you out to dinner. Are you free tonight?"

"No, I'm not," she said so fast it surprised even her.

"In other words I'd be stepping on Eli's territory."

Suddenly she heard her cell phone ring. The timing couldn't have been more perfect. "Mr. Shapiro? I have to take another call and can't talk now. I'm sorry. Good-bye."

Brianna hung up before clicking on her cell without checking the caller ID. "Hello?" she said.

"Hi, it's Lindsay."

"Oh, I'm so glad it's you." She leaned on the counter in relief.

"What's wrong?"

"Nothing really. I just hung up on a nuisance caller."

"Oh dear."

It was too late to worry that she'd offended the bank manager her uncle did business with. Don Shapiro had been way out of line the first time she'd met him, let alone now. "What's new? How's the pregnant mom feeling?"

"I'm fine, thanks, but I thought you might want to know what Ken told me before he left for work."

Brianna went on alert. "Go on."

"While he was on duty last night, Eli Clayton brought his little girl into the ER at four in the morning with a bad case of croup."

"Oh no—" Poor Libby… Brianna's body broke out in perspiration.

"That's what *I* said. Ken knew I'd met them when you and I went out for dinner recently. He said she's been hospitalized. I don't know anything else, but I thought that maybe you'd want to know, if you hadn't heard already."

"I do!" she cried. "I'm going over to the hospital right now. I'll get back to you later. Thanks so much for letting me know." She clicked off.

It was closing time anyway and Brianna quickly closed up the store, and then got in her truck and drove to the hospital a mile away. She took the elevator to the pediatric wing and approached the male nurse working on a chart at the nursing station.

"Excuse me. Do you know if Libby Clayton is still a patient here?"

The nurse lifted his head. "She is. Are you a relative?"

"No. I'm Brianna Frost, a friend of the Clayton family. May I see her?"

"Sure. She's in room W1124 down that hall."

Brianna thanked him and walked past five doors. When she opened door to Libby's room, she saw Eli walking around, holding his sleeping daughter in his arms. Her breathing sounded noisy. It wrenched her heart.

Eli looked across the short distance and stared as if he couldn't believe Brianna was standing there.

Her mouth had gone dry. "Lindsay called me at work. Her husband told her you'd brought Libby in."

"That's right. He was the attending physician."

"Yes. Is it okay that I've come?" she whispered without moving.

"There's no one we'd rather see." His words filled her with relief. "Please, sit down."

Brianna took off her parka and hung it over the back of a chair. "Is she better than she was in the middle of the night?"

"Yes, even though it sounds bad. They took an X-ray and gave her medication in the emergency room. The pediatrician advised keeping her overnight just in case. Around seven this morning she was given an oral corticosteroid to reduce the inflammation and swelling. If all continues to go well, I'll be able to take her home tonight."

"Thank Heaven. Do you know how she got it?"

"No. It's a virus. Hers grew worse, but at least she's resting more comfortably now."

"I take it you haven't left her for a second. Has your mother been here?"

He nodded. "You just missed her and Wymon. They went out to buy a cool mist steamer for her room."

"I'm glad they've been here for you. Have you had dinner yet?"

"The orderly left a tray, but I haven't touched it."

She noticed it on one of the tables. "Would you let me hold her so you can eat?"

"You want to?"

"I'd love it." She'd tried without success to keep the tremor out of her voice.

"You're sure?" he asked. The blue of his eyes darkened with emotion. "Even though you said good-bye to me?"

She deserved that. "I was upset that night," Brianna answered honestly. "Your daughter is so precious, Eli. Of course I want to hold her. I'll try not to wake her up."

"Don't worry about it." He walked over and placed Libby in her arms. She was viscerally aware of the difference between his hard-muscled physique beneath his white T-shirt and jeans, and the tiny slip of a thing that was his daughter, dressed in a fuzzy onesie dotted with teddy bears.

The motion caused Libby's eyelids to flutter open. Her blue eyes, so much like her father's, stared up at Brianna.

"Hi, darling. Do you remember me? I'm Brianna."

"Bree," she croaked out the first part of her name and squirmed to sit up.

"Yes. Bree." She helped her to get up. The little girl put her arms around her neck and clung to her. Brianna held her against her heart and felt the breaths she took. "I'm so glad you're feeling better." She rocked her back and forth, loving the feeling of those arms holding on to her.

Though he sported a slight beard and looked exhausted, Eli's face broke into a smile as he stood there watching them. "I do believe you're the reason she's suddenly acting so normal."

Brianna smiled up at him. "Her daddy is all the medicine she needs, but you'd better sit down and have something to eat so you don't pass out from fatigue."

"I look that bad, huh?"

She averted her eyes. Brianna didn't dare tell him how good he looked to her, even now.

He walked over to the table and lifted the cover off the dinner plate before sitting down a few feet from her to eat.

Libby swung her head around and pointed at him. "Dada."

"Yup! That's me, sweetheart." He handed her half of his roll. She reached for it and took a bite.

Brianna squeezed her. "It looks like you're hungry."

He nodded. "That's a good sign she's getting better."

He'd just finished his meal when a man entered the room. Eli stood. "Dr. Ennis? This is my friend, Brianna Frost. Her uncle owns Frosts' Western Saddlery."

The older man nodded. "Of course. I've been in there many times." He walked over and hunkered down in front of Brianna. "Don't move. Just keep holding her while I check her lungs." He put the stethoscope to his ears and moved it around. Libby tried to squirm away.

In a minute the doctor got to his feet. "It's clear she's improving, Eli. You can take her home and keep the cool steam going. Sleep in her room tonight to listen for any changes in her breathing. I'll go out to the desk and sign the release papers."

Eli looked relieved. "That's the news I've been waiting for. Thanks, Dr. Ennis."

"My pleasure. The miracle is that children rally fast." He smiled at Brianna. "It was nice to meet you. Libby seems very fond of you."

"She's a darling."

"When she was born, she was the cutest baby in the nursery. Now she's even cuter." He patted Eli's shoulder. "Call the office tomorrow and give me a report."

The two men walked out into the hallway.

Brianna kissed Libby's cheek. "The doctor's right. With that heart-shaped face, you *are* the cutest thing in the world."

"Let me just check her diaper and then we can leave." Eli had come back in and plucked her out of Brianna's arms. His daughter protested as he carried her over to the crib.

"I'll find her parka." It was hanging in the closet along with his sheepskin jacket. "If you want, when we go down to the lobby, I can hold her while you get your truck and warm it up."

"I'd like to take you up on that on one condition." He snapped up Libby's sleeper suit and put the parka on her. Brianna's heart thudded while she waited for the rest. "That you follow us back to the ranch in your truck and help me put her to bed. Now that you've made an appearance, she's going to be very upset if you leave. But if you have other plans..."

"No. I'll just phone my aunt and tell her I'll be home late tonight so they won't worry," she said, hoping her face didn't give away just how happy she was that he had asked.

"That's good to hear." Eli shrugged into his jacket and then reached for Libby. "Come on, sweetheart. We're all going home."

We're all going home. The sound of that sent a thrill through Brianna's body.

A hospital orderly appeared with a wheelchair.

"Really?" Eli questioned. The look on his face was comical.

"Sorry," the man said. "Hospital rules."

Eli sat in the chair and held his daughter. One dark brow lifted. "You'd think I'd just given birth," he muttered.

Libby chuckled as she walked alongside them to the elevator.

THE WOMAN KEEPING pace with them looked sensational in her melon-colored sweater and designer jeans. Eli felt like a fraud being wheeled out in the chair, but Brianna's gentle laughter sweetened the experience.

"I'll hold her," Brianna said when they reached the hospital entrance. Libby went right into her arms with no fuss. Eli thanked the orderly and took off for the parking lot. He started up the truck and brought it around to the entrance. When he felt it was warm enough, he left the engine running and went inside to get Libby. But the second he took her from Brianna's arms, she started to cry.

"It's okay, sweetheart. She's coming home with us."

Brianna walked with them out to the truck and waited while he strapped her inside and gave her some plastic, colored keys to play with.

"I'll see you in a minute, Libby. I promise." She kissed her cheeks before he shut the door on her croaky cries.

"Where's your truck?"

"Right down this row. I'll hurry."

"Drive safely. I couldn't handle another emergency tonight."

"I'll be right behind you."

Eli waited for Brianna and then pulled out of the parking lot and headed for the ranch. His daughter whimpered while he kept an eye on Brianna's truck in the rearview mirror. Before he'd been able to phone her Sunday evening after his trip to Thompson Falls, his daughter's condition had deteriorated. On Monday she'd gone from bad to worse. When he'd seen Brianna enter the hospital room tonight, he'd thought he was hallucinating.

Without this crisis bringing them together unexpectedly, there was no telling how long it would have taken him to get Brianna to talk to him. He silently thanked her friend Lindsay for letting her know what had happened.

For some reason, Libby had responded to Brianna from the very first time she'd seen her at the gem shop, and those feelings were obviously reciprocated. Otherwise she would never have come to the hospital after telling him good-bye. Now she'd willingly agreed to come back to his house.

When they reached the driveway, she pulled up her truck alongside his. They both got out. His family had left the porch light on. He went around to pluck Libby from her car seat, while Brianna gathered the diaper bag and little toys that had fallen on the drive over, and then they walked inside the house.

Wymon had made a fire and left more lights on to welcome them. Eli carried Libby through the living room and down the hall to the nursery. The room held a twin bed, a dresser, her crib and a rocking chair.

"Is Sarah here?"

He removed Libby's parka and put her in bed with the white polar bear she loved. "No. She goes home on weekends. On Sunday, when I realized Libby was sick and I'd have to stay home from work on Monday, I told her not to come in for a few days. I'm planning to stay home tomorrow, too."

After taking off his jacket, he switched on the new steamer his mother had set up and turned to Brianna. She'd removed her parka, too, and had put it on the bed with the diaper bag and other things. "If you'll stay with her, I'll go in the kitchen and get her a bottle of apple juice."

"Mmm, juice. That sounds good, doesn't it, Libby."

His little girl had gotten to her feet and clung to the crib railing. "Dada," she called to him as he left the room.

When he returned a minute later, he discovered Brianna holding her in the rocking chair. To his relief he could tell her coughing was much less severe and she seemed animated.

Eli walked over and handed the bottle to her. She put it right in her mouth and drank. Brianna looked up at him. "I think she's happy to be back in her own room."

That wasn't all she was happy about. "Yup. There's no place like home." Eli reached for a book sitting on the small pile on the dresser. "This is her favorite. When she's through drinking, she'll love reading it with you."

"Ooh. *Goodnight Moon.* Can you say *moon,* Libby? Moooooooooon."

Libby pulled the bottle away and he heard her say "Mooooooo," in a croaky voice.

The moment was so precious that both he and Brianna burst into laughter. "That's her sixth word," he said.

Their gazes collided. "You've been counting them?"

"Yes. She can say *Dada, Nana* and *Sol.* Around you, she has now said *Bree, bye* and *moo.* I'll have to get her a cow so she knows the difference."

"Maybe you'd better buy a wolf, too. You know. Howling at the mooooooooooooooooon?" As Eli chuckled and Libby said the word again. Brianna kissed the top of her head. "You're a very smart girl, you know that? But I think it's time you went to bed."

Eli gathered Libby in his arms, aware of Brianna's sweet fragrance on her. He lay her down in the crib to change her diaper one more time. He didn't realize

Brianna had left the nursery until after he'd finally gotten his daughter to sleep. Leaving the small night-light on, he tiptoed out of the room to the bathroom across the hall to wash his hands.

His breath caught when he walked into the living room and saw Brianna sitting by the fireplace, her pale hair illuminated by the glow from the flames. She appeared deep in thought.

"Brianna?"

She turned to him and stood. Her parka lay across the end of the couch. "I hope your crisis is over."

"I'm sure it is, and you had a part in her fast recovery, but there's another crisis I need to deal with now."

He could tell she was the slightest bit out of breath. That was how he felt whenever he was around her.

"What's wrong?"

"You and I need time alone together. By Sunday, Libby ought to be much better. Mom will want to spend time with her. I'd like to take you out for dinner and talk. It's important. Last Saturday Libby and I went to see my ex-wife."

Her face blanched. "She saw Libby?"

"Yes. There are things I need to tell you about what happened. If I come pick you up at five, will you be ready?"

Several seconds passed before she nodded.

Now he could swallow. "It's getting late. If you'll wait a moment, I'll phone Wymon and ask him to follow you home."

"Thank you, but please don't. We don't live that far apart."

He rubbed the back of his neck in frustration. "Then will you let me put my phone number on your cell? I want you to call me when you've reached your uncle's."

"All right." They exchanged numbers. Before he could help her, she'd already put on her parka and started for the door.

Eli walked her out to her truck and made certain she was safe. He tapped on the window so she'd lower it. "You coming to the hospital tonight meant more to me than you know. I guess you don't need to be told Libby was a new little girl after you walked in the room."

"I'm glad she's doing so much better," Brianna said. "Take care of yourself, Eli. I'll see you on Sunday at five."

Her warm breath in the cold night air made him want to reach through that window and pull her into his arms. He hoped she was having the same feelings and thought maybe that was why it took her a whole minute to start the engine.

Eli stood there and watched until her truck disappeared around the bend. A new chapter in his life had begun. He could feel it. Though dead on his feet from worry and lack of sleep, he felt exhilarated as he walked back into the house to get ready for bed.

Five minutes later his phone rang. She couldn't have reached her uncle's yet. Something had to be wrong. He picked up without checking the caller ID. "Brianna?"

"Brianna, huh?" his brother teased. "So that's what

has been going on while I've been getting the tar knocked out of me on the circuit!"

"Toly!"

"Yeah. You *do* remember me, but you sound out of breath." Eli needed to calm down. "Mom said Libby had been in the hospital with croup. Is she all right?"

"Yes. I brought her home earlier tonight."

"That's a relief. So who's Brianna?"

His heart raced. "Brianna Frost is a woman I recently met."

"Hmm. She must be very new if I haven't met her."

"She actually came to the rodeo with her aunt and uncle to watch you and Mills."

"You're talking Clark Frost?"

"Clark's her uncle. She works at the saddlery."

"Is she blonde?"

He blinked. "Yes."

"Then she's the one Asa Harding has a crush on!"

Eli had to bite his tongue. Asa and every other man in Stevensville.

"He came to see me in the stock pen after the rodeo and told me about this gorgeous babe he met when he went to buy some new shirts. How did *you* meet her?"

"At the gem shop. Mom was showing her some stones. I went up there to get Libby. Listen, Toly— it's good to hear from you and congratulations on another first last Saturday night, but I've got to hit the hay because I'm ready to pass out. I'll call you tomorrow and we'll talk."

"I'm going to hold you to that and you know why." They clicked off.

Yup. Eli was afraid he did.

The Clayton family had been worried about Eli for a long time. He knew Toly was shocked to hear another woman's name pass through his lips besides Tessa's. There'd been a huge change in Eli's life.

While he stood there in a daze, the phone rang again. This time he checked the caller ID before clicking on. "Brianna? Are you home?"

"I promised I'd call. I'm in the house. How's Libby?"

Libby who? For a moment Eli's mind had been in a different place. "She's still asleep and sounding better."

"Oh, that makes me so happy! Now you go to bed or you'll end up in the hospital."

"Yes, ma'am."

Her chuckle was the last sound he heard before she hung up. That chuckle invaded his body and accompanied him to the twin bed in Libby's room, where he collapsed as soon as his head touched the pillow.

Chapter Six

On Saturday after store hours, Brianna tried on the Wrangler two-piece suit in formfitting denim that had just come in. With a white scooped-neck top underneath, the outfit seemed perfect. She wrote up the invoice and paid cash for it using the discount her uncle gave her. Since coming to Montana, she hadn't bought anything new for herself and thought it was time.

Her uncle figured out why after he saw her walk into the living room Sunday evening carrying her coat. Her aunt was in the kitchen fixing their dinner. "Where are you going?"

"To dinner with Eli Clayton."

An odd expression broke out on his face, reminding her of her dad when he was pondering something serious. "Somehow I didn't expect Eli to come out the winner of the Clayton brothers. So it was *Eli* all along, not Roce."

"I—I didn't intend to see him again," she stammered, "but Lindsay told me his little girl was in the hospital with croup, so I went to visit her."

"And now he wants to thank you."

"Yes." She wasn't ready to talk about it yet.

"I take it she's better now." He cocked his head. "Are you sure about going with him? From what I understand, he's the complicated one."

Complicated?

"Clark," her aunt called out. She'd just walked into the living room with Taffy at her heels. "What a question to ask. Dinner's ready. Come in the dining room and let Brianna do her own thing. That suit looks terrific on you, by the way."

Her aunt Joanne gave her a hug before reaching for her husband's hand. The gorgeous pink sapphire on her finger flashed in the lamplight, reminding Brianna of the first time she'd met Eli.

Not thirty seconds later the doorbell rang. Brianna put on her coat and hurried to the foyer, thinking about what her uncle had just said. When she opened the door, Eli's striking blue eyes swept down the length of her, making her heart ricochet all over the place.

"Thanks for being ready on time. I couldn't have waited any longer." The things he said gave her a fluttery feeling in her chest. Eli wore a tan jacket and cream shirt with beige pants. Today he was clean shaven and smelled wonderful. He walked her out to the truck. When he helped her get in, she noticed he'd left his overcoat on the backseat.

"How's Libby?"

"If you'd seen her toddling around the ranch house a little while ago, you would never know she'd been so sick. There's only been one problem."

She dared a look at him.

"Every so often she says 'Bree' to me. Libby keeps looking for you."

"She does?" Eli shouldn't have told her that.

"Surely you're not surprised." He started the engine and they left. "I hope you like Italian food. The Italian owner cooks the food himself. I've never been to Italy, but I don't see how the food would taste any better there."

"That sounds good to me." Last week she hadn't thought she'd be seeing Eli again. Now here she was going out to eat with him. She shouldn't be this elated, but she couldn't help it.

Before long they reached the small restaurant and were shown to a table. "You look stunning," he murmured after removing her coat.

So did he. "Thank you."

They were fed one delicious course after another. While they chatted about their work and sipped coffee, he said, "Thanks to what you said, my trip to Thompson Falls accomplished two things."

The sudden change of topic caused her pulse to race. She stared at him. "What do you mean?"

"You told me not to stop trying to win my wife back. I took your advice and drove down to Thompson Falls with Libby to see Tessa again. After a year I was curious to find out what would happen when Tessa saw us again. But the woman who answered the door looked through me as if I weren't there. As for Libby, Tessa had no desire to hold her. I promised she'd never see me again."

Brianna groaned. "I'm sorry."

"Don't be. She was a stranger to me and has been for a long time, but I didn't want to admit that our marriage was one of those that didn't make it. That was the reason why I wore my ring as long as I did."

"I do understand, Eli."

"Then you're one woman in a million."

She shook her head. "Hardly."

"The important thing here is that I know in my soul it wasn't anyone's fault. The doctor can't give me the exact reason for her illness, but it wasn't something preventable."

"Of course not," she whispered.

"I returned home a new man and planned to call you Sunday evening, but by then Libby was so sick that I was preoccupied. I'd like to thank your friend for telling you she was in the hospital. It meant the world to me and Libby that you came."

Brianna drank the rest of her coffee. This was the time for honesty. "It meant a lot to me, too."

He leaned forward. "I hope by now you understand that I've asked you to dinner because I want to start over again with you. Let's not have any secrets or concerns that aren't out in the open. If there's something you need to tell me that would hold you back from being with me, I want to hear it."

She cleared her throat, shaken by his earnestness. "Well, I'm not involved with another man, as I told you at the restaurant."

One brow lifted. "Not even Asa Harding?"

"Mr. Harding?"

His eyes danced. "Toly told me Asa has a crush on you."

"That's news to me. He's been in the store a couple of times, that's all."

"All it takes is seeing you once... Take it from a cowboy who knows."

Heat filled her cheeks. "He asked me to go a movie with him, but I told him I was busy that night."

"Were you?" he asked.

"No."

"The poor dude."

Brianna smiled. "He's nice, but—"

"But the spark wasn't there?"

She lowered her eyes. "Can we change the subject?"

"Gladly. I want to know your future plans."

So did she, but everything was a blur right now. "They're in flux."

"In other words they could change at any minute."

Brianna raised her head. "Maybe not that fast."

His eyes narrowed on her face. She saw no mirth in them. "In case you were wondering, my plans are fixed. Ranching's my life and the Sapphire Mountains are my home. If you have any intention of going back to California or getting a job somewhere else right away, I need to know so I won't be blindsided when it happens."

"*Eli*—"

"Eli, what?" he demanded. "You know what I'm saying."

She took a shaky breath. "I'm very happy living with my aunt and uncle."

"Until…"

He was driving her crazy. "Until, I don't know!"

Eli broke into laughter. "That answer will do for now. Tell me something. Does your uncle ever give you part of a day off?"

"If I ask, he tells me to take whatever time I need."

"That's a great boss. Could you plan for this coming Tuesday? Say two o'clock when I'm done with my ranching chores?"

"What do you have in mind?"

"Have you ever gone skiing?"

"Only when I'm here in winter. I have a pair of skis and boots at my aunt and uncle's. I've gone twice so far since I've been here."

"Terrific. I thought we'd go skiing at the Snowbowl outside Missoula. We ought to be able to get in a few hours and then have dinner. Sarah will be there for Libby so we won't have to worry if we get back late."

Skiing with Eli sounded wonderful. Doing *anything* with him sounded like Heaven. "I'd love to go skiing."

"Good. Then it's settled. Come on. I'll drive you home. Though I'd love to spend the entire evening with you, I want to be able to say good-night to Libby. Mom is watching her, but she's been a little needy since her hospital stay."

"I can understand that. She's lucky to have such a devoted father. Let's go."

Brianna decided he was a breed apart from most

men. She still found it incredible that his ex-wife's condition was too severe for her to want a life with him. But tonight Eli had made it clear Tessa was a part of the past. At this point Brianna would have to operate on faith that she wasn't making a mistake by continuing to see him.

Eli saw her to the door.

"Thank you for a fantastic dinner." In the dim porch light she glimpsed banked fires in his eyes, but he still didn't try to kiss her. She wanted him to. Badly. So much for her deciding to take things slowly. *You're a mess, Brianna.*

He squeezed her arm. "See you on Tuesday afternoon. I can't promise I'll survive until then."

She laughed quietly but entered the house breathless. Much as she wanted to go straight to her room, she stopped by the den first where her aunt and uncle were watching television. Taffy limped over so she could rub her head.

"Hi! I'm home." Anticipating the next question, she said, "I had a wonderful time. Eli asked me to go skiing with him on Tuesday."

"That sounds fun," her aunt commented.

"I think so, too. Uncle Clark, would it be all right if I take off work at two?"

"Of course."

For once her uncle was unusually quiet, but maybe he was just too caught up in the movie they were watching to ask any more questions.

"Great. Well, I'm going to bed. See you in the morning."

"Good night, honey."

She went to her room not at all sure how she'd make it to Tuesday afternoon.

"SARAH? I'M BACK!"

After inspecting the cattle with Wymon and the stock workers, Eli hurried into the house at one o'clock on Tuesday to shower and change. He'd been living for today.

"Libby and I are building a castle!"

He found them in the nursery on the floor. "Dada!" Libby had blocks in both hands that she lifted to show him.

Eli hunkered down next to his daughter. "Well, look at you." He kissed the top of her head.

Sarah smiled. "She loves building things."

"Maybe I've got myself an engineer."

While Libby was busy building stuff, he got ready for his date and loaded his ski equipment into the back of the truck. Figuring it would be easier if Libby didn't know he was going, he left the house to pick up Brianna without saying good-bye. Sarah knew he'd be home late.

The best thing he'd done in a year was hire a nanny. He should have done it long before now, but he hadn't wanted to go into debt. Eli had worked hard to save money and now a new sense of freedom filled his being as he drove into town and pulled up in the Frosts' driveway.

The sight of Brianna in her black ski jacket and form-fitting ski pants nearly knocked him back on his behind. Her womanly shape filled his vision to the exclusion of all else.

"Bring your cowboy hat. You're going to need it later," he said.

"That's sounds interesting."

After she fetched it, he carried her ski equipment to the truck while she climbed inside the cab. Then they drove away. He put her hat in the backseat by his. Eli shot her a penetrating glance. "I feel eighteen again."

"Is that good or bad?" she teased.

"What do you think?"

"Was that a happy time for you?"

It seemed an odd question, or maybe not. "Let's put it this way. At that age I came to appreciate a fine-looking woman. But I can tell you right now there was no one like you around."

"I don't believe it."

"Just ask any of the guys who've been coming in and out of the saddlery nonstop since you arrived in Stevensville."

"You're very good on a woman's ego. But when you see what a klutz I am on the slopes, you'll have to reassess your thinking."

He raised an eyebrow. "Did I tell you I was once a bull rider, not a skier?"

"I'll reserve judgment until we call an ambulance for you."

"No, thank you. One hospital visit this month for any reason is enough."

She laughed gently. "I agree. How is Libby now?"

"Perfect. I left her constructing a castle out of blocks with Sarah."

"I've noticed she has an incredible attention span for her age."

He darted another glance at her. "I've noticed she's crazy about you. If you can prevail on your uncle to let you off work this coming Saturday, I want you to come to the house for part of the day. Libby will be ecstatic. I'll do the cooking and we'll roast marshmallows in the fireplace."

Eli knew he was getting ahead of himself, but being with Brianna felt so right, he couldn't stop thinking and planning. He was waiting for her answer.

"I'll arrange to do a split shift with him and leave after lunch. Mornings are the busiest time on Saturdays. He'll get a few customers in the afternoon, but we usually close up early."

"Then it's settled." Eli reached over and grasped her hand for a few minutes.

The sky stayed overcast with more snow forecast to fall by evening. He'd buy them half-day passes and hopefully they'd get some skiing in before that happened. "If I ever had to go into another profession, I'd like it to be photography. I'd take pictures of Montana in winter," he mused.

"Everything does look like a Christmas card. It's so beautiful here."

"Don't you miss California, though?"

She was looking out the side window. "I haven't

allowed myself to think much about it. At first I was in denial over my parents' deaths."

"And now?" he whispered.

"I miss them like crazy, but I've finally accepted that they're gone and life goes on. When I talk to my brother now, he accuses me of having forgotten him. That could never happen, of course."

"Has he been to visit your aunt and uncle since you came?"

"No. They've begged him. If you knew my brother, you'd realize he's such a responsible person that he's afraid to leave the farm, even for a short period of time. In some ways he reminds me of you and how dedicated you are. I've noticed how you keep watch over everything down at the ranch along with your brothers. He, too, has farm workers he's responsible for."

Her compliments warmed him. "You must miss him a lot."

"I do, but my aunt and uncle fill a big void. Clark and Dad are so much alike. As for Doug, he has his wife, Carol, so we're all doing better."

Yes, we are. I know I am.

They reached the crowded ski resort and got in line for the double chair lift. When they reached the top, Brianna turned to him. "I'm a slow skier. If you want to go ahead, please don't let me stop you."

He shook his head. "I want to ski with you, so you set the pace. Are you ready?"

"Yes. But you'll be sorry." She lowered her goggles and started down the slope. He stayed near her side until they reached the bottom. "Forgive me for being so slow, Eli."

"Please don't apologize. You have excellent technique."

"Thank you. I love being out in nature with you. Let's go up again."

Halfway to the top, a cold wind kicked up. She smiled nervously at him. "I think the storm front is moving in faster than predicted."

"I agree. We'll make another run and see what happens."

After they'd made two more descents without incident, it started to snow. He saw that Brianna was anxious. "You ready to head into Missoula for dinner?"

She nodded, her relief obvious. When they reached the truck, he opened the passenger door for her. "Let me help you."

Needing to touch her, he grasped her around the waist. As her body brushed against his, a wave of desire spread through him. It was so strong that he pulled her close and her head fell back. The moment was magical. With the snow coming down, all he could see were her jewel-like blue eyes and sculpted mouth, a temptation he could no longer resist.

"I've been wanting to do this since the first time we met," he whispered fiercely before covering her mouth with his own. Her luscious warmth, combined with the cold air and snow, increased his desire. He forgot where they were as he deepened their kiss. She clung to him, causing his heart to race. In that instant he knew she wanted him just as badly and they kissed each other close to senselessness.

Having lost all track of time, he was eventually brought back to his senses when someone passing by let out a wolf whistle. With Brianna in his arms, he was in danger of being totally out of control. For a first kiss, they'd gone way beyond what was wise, let alone what was decent in a public place.

It was like the first night he'd laid eyes on her at the gem shop. The sight of her had stirred his senses to such a degree that he hadn't been the same since. All along he'd known that if he ever started kissing her, he wouldn't be able to stop. He'd never felt this way about any woman. His attraction to his ex-wife had grown slowly. The excitement Brianna whipped up inside him staggered him.

With sheer strength of will, he lifted his mouth from hers and could hear his own ragged breathing. "Up you go." This time he put her inside and shut the door before he could clasp her to him again.

Once behind the wheel, he shut the door and started the engine. She'd pulled off her headband. Her blond hair glowed with a life all its own. It was impossible to tear his eyes away from her.

"I feel like a good steak. How about you?"

"That sounds good." But her response told him she was miles away in the same world where he'd been moments ago. Eli needed to channel his energy in a different way and knew exactly the place to take her.

The snow continued to come down. She fixed her makeup and brushed out her hair. Within a half hour they arrived at Rudy's, the best steak house in Missoula. He reached for their cowboy hats. Once they'd gotten out of the truck, they put them on and he grasped her arm to guide her inside.

"I hope you know how to line dance. If you don't, I'll teach you. They have a great band here." This way he could touch her but would have to control himself.

Her eyes lit up. "My aunt taught me. She and Uncle Clark go country dancing a lot. I love it."

The good news just kept coming.

They were shown to a table around the dance floor and removed their parkas. Every male in the place eyed her in her tight black cashmere sweater. He couldn't blame them, but thanked providence he'd gotten there first.

After being served some tapas for hors d'oeuvres, he led her out to the dance floor and they joined a dozen people sashaying to "Baby Likes to Rock It." Her aunt had taught her well. Dancing with Brianna excited him to no end.

They went back to the table to enjoy the main course and then returned to the floor and danced for close to an hour. Eli had forgotten he could be this happy. Her smiles let him know she was feeling the same way. But before long, he wanted her to himself and suggested they leave. He helped her put on her parka, loving the fragrant scent of her skin and hair.

Their stomachs filled with good food, the drive back to Stevensville in the snowstorm seemed just as magical as the rest of the night. Encased in the cab together, alone in the darkness, Eli felt he had everything he wanted.

"I guess I don't need to tell you how much this day has meant to me. There's only one problem."

After a brief silence, she said, "I don't think I want to know what it is."

"That's because you know what I'm going to say."

"Eli…"

"It's too soon to have the kind of feelings I have for you. I know it, and you know it. Tonight I want to take you home with me for good. You'd be lying if you told me you didn't feel the same way."

"I'll admit I'm overwhelmed with emotions right now."

"Whether you want to hear it or not, I've fallen in love with you." He detected a slight gasp. "I don't need to hear all the arguments floating in your head. I know them by heart and can just imagine what your brother would say.

"'It's too soon, Brianna. Eli Clayton has just come out of a marriage that couldn't work. He couldn't possibly know what he wants yet. He has a little daughter. You've never been married. You're still grieving the loss of our parents. You're a California girl and are only visiting our aunt and uncle for a season. You need to come home and deserve to meet a man with no baggage.'"

She straightened in the seat. "Everyone has baggage, Eli."

"Not like mine."

"Maybe not exactly. Why don't you tell me the

whole truth and admit you'd be worried to take on a girl like me with no experience? You've been married and have a child. I'm sure I don't measure up to your expectations, not like—"

"Tessa?" he interrupted her. "You're right. You're not at all like Tessa, who was afraid of her own shadow. I didn't know that at first. When she begged me never to go back to bull riding again, I thought that was a natural concern of some people. Later I took her skiing, but she couldn't bring herself to get on the lift, which surprised me.

"After we got married and moved in to my late grandparents' house, fear turned out to be her middle name. She liked to go dancing but not line dancing, where she felt like she was on display. It was clear Tessa needed to be home where she could be in control of her world and she begged for us to start a family. I'd wanted to wait, but I could see a baby would fulfill her."

"Oh, Eli... How hard."

"Her pregnancy made her so happy, despite her morning sickness, that I was overjoyed. We planned out the nursery and got everything ready. Little did I know Libby's arrival would bring completely new fears.

"If you have more questions about her, go ahead and ask. But you have to know I don't measure you against anyone else. You are a constant surprise in ways that make me thankful I've met you."

Eli pulled into the Frosts' snow-covered driveway.

FREE Merchandise and a Cash Reward† are 'in the Cards' for you!

Dear Reader,

We're giving away FREE MERCHANDISE and a CASH REWARD!

Seriously, we'd like to reward you for reading this novel by giving you **FREE MERCHANDISE** worth over $20 retail plus a CASH REWARD! And no purchase is necessary!

You see the Jack of Hearts sticker above? Paste that sticker in the box on the Free Merchandise Voucher inside. Return the Voucher today... and we'll send you Free Merchandise plus a Cash Reward!

Thanks again for reading one of our novels—and enjoy your Free Merchandise and Cash Reward with our compliments!

Pam Powers

Pam Powers

P.S. Look inside to see what Free Merchandise is **"in the cards"** for you!

We'd like to send you two free books like the one you are enjoying now. Your two books have a combined price of over $10 retail, but they are yours to keep absolutely FREE! We'll even send you 2 wonderful surprise gifts and a Cash Reward†. You can't lose!

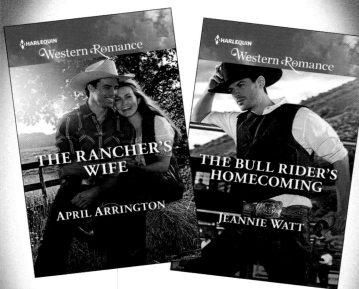

REMEMBER: Your Free Merchandise, consisting of **2 Free Books** and **2 Free Gifts**, is worth over **$20** retail! Plus we'll send you a **Cash Reward** (it's a dollar) which is really the icing on the cake because it's in addition to your FREE Merchandise! No purchase is necessary, so please send for your Free Merchandise today.

Get TWO FREE GIFTS!
We'll also send you 2 wonderful FREE GIFTS (worth about $10 retail), in addition to your 2 Free books and Cash Reward!

Visit us at:
www.ReaderService.com

YOUR FREE MERCHANDISE INCLUDES...
2 FREE Books **AND** 2 FREE Mystery Gifts
PLUS you'll get a Cash Reward†

FREE MERCHANDISE VOUCHER

2 FREE BOOKS and 2 FREE GIFTS

Please send my Free Merchandise, consisting of
2 Free Books and **2 Free Mystery Gifts** PLUS my
Cash Reward. I understand that I am under no
obligation to buy anything, as explained
on the back of this card.

154/354 HDL GLTA

Please Print

FIRST NAME

LAST NAME

ADDRESS

APT.#   CITY

STATE/PROV.   ZIP/POSTAL CODE

NO PURCHASE NECESSARY!

WR-N16-FMC15

"Meeting you has changed my world, too, Eli. So much that I don't know myself anymore."

Unable to stand it any longer, he got out of the truck and walked around to her side. After opening the door, he pulled her into his arms. "I need this again or I'll never make it until Saturday."

Once more he knew rapture as they gave each other kiss after kiss under falling snow that left their hair and clothing damp. But he wasn't aware of anything except the feel of the fabulous flesh-and-blood woman embracing him as if she would never let him go. To experience this kind of passion seemed nothing short of a miracle.

When she pulled away long enough to catch her breath, she cried, "You look like a snowman."

"To tell you the truth, with the heat we've created, I'm surprised the snow hasn't run off both of us." He covered her mouth once more before freeing her from his grip. "You'd better run to the porch while I'm still willing to let you go. I'll get your ski equipment."

After gathering it up, he put everything down on her porch and clasped her to him one more time. "I don't want to let you go, but I have to. Just be warned that on Saturday, things will be different. I'll expect you around one or one-thirty."

"I'll be there."

He gave her another swift kiss and walked back to the truck without turning around.

Chapter Seven

Taffy was waiting when Brianna entered the house and removed her parka. Then her uncle came walking toward her. She didn't have to guess what he was thinking. Her disheveled hair, her flushed cheeks and swollen lips told him everything.

"I saw headlights in the driveway. I'll bring in your equipment. Why don't you go rest by the fire?"

Yup. He'd been waiting up for her. She sensed a talk coming on. Because she loved him so much, she didn't resent him behaving like a father, even if she was twenty-three.

While she waited for him, she took off her boots and stood in front of the hearth. The only parts of her body not burning up were her feet.

"Were you able to get in some skiing before the storm hit?"

She turned toward him. "Yes. We did four runs. Eli is such a good skier, I can't believe he wasn't an alpine champion."

"He was an even greater bull rider."

She nodded. "I'm sure of that, but he insists Toly is

the true champion of the family. After we left the ski resort, we went to Rudy's for dinner and line dancing. I don't think there's anything the guy can't do. I had the time of my life."

Her uncle scrutinized her. "Your eyes are shining with a light I've never seen before. I dare say my niece is in love."

She took a steadying breath. "I *know* I am."

"Brianna—"

"Yes?"

He was unusually hesitant. "Nothing."

"Come on, Uncle Clark. You didn't wait up this late for nothing."

"I don't have the right."

"Yes, you do. What are you trying to tell me?"

"That your aunt and I love you and want you to be happy."

"I know you're concerned. You told me Eli was the complicated one of the Clayton boys. What did you mean by that?"

He shifted his weight. "It's something his father once said to me."

Brianna swallowed hard. "What was that?"

"Everything always came easily to Eli. For that reason his dad worried there'd come a time when he had to face something all his talents couldn't fix."

She folded her arms in front of her waist. "When did he tell you this? After Eli's marriage to Tessa?"

"No, before. He came into the store one day to buy some boots and mentioned that Eli was getting married."

"Wasn't he happy about it?"

"Not exactly. He felt uneasy because Eli and his fiancée hadn't known each other long and he thought they were rushing into it."

"You don't think that he was just a loving father who was worried about losing his son?"

"No. He had a real concern."

"In other words he felt Eli wasn't ready but didn't give you the exact reason why."

"I suppose that's it."

She thought of how wonderful Eli was with his daughter. "Who *is* truly ready when it comes to marriage?"

He took a deep breath. "I'm sure I don't know."

"It seems to me Eli did everything to try to make his marriage work and has proven himself to be a great dad. If his father were alive, I should think he'd be proud of him."

"Of course he would be. Honey?" His eyes looked at her with pleading. "Forgive me for saying anything."

Brianna gave him a big hug. "Thank you for caring so much. Good night."

She hurried to her room to get ready for bed. But no matter how hard she tried, she couldn't throw off her uncle's concern. Brianna believed he'd told her the whole truth as he knew it. So if she wanted to know the rest, she would have to ask Eli why his father had such reservations about his marriage that he'd even discussed them with her uncle.

For the remainder of the week her uncle kept mum

on the subject. Eli phoned her at work the next day to be certain she was still on for Saturday. He made another call on Friday while they were vaccinating the herd.

"When I left the house this morning, I told Libby you would be coming to our house tomorrow. It doesn't matter how much she understood—one thing was clear. She kept running around saying, 'Bree—Bree!' You've made a real impression on her. Neither one of us can wait."

"I'm looking forward to it, too," she said. "See you then."

After work that day, Brianna called Lindsay and they decided to go shopping for a present for Libby. Her pregnant friend was delighted by the idea and they met at one of the stores selling educational gifts.

They found a box of twelve different-colored moons. Six were full moons—pancake-sized and about a half-inch thick, while the other six were half moons in the same colors. All had adorable faces. Brianna knew Libby would love them. She also bought a coloring book of cartoon moon drawings and a pack of crayons.

Lindsay found a mobile of the solar system for the crib she and her husband had set up. Her friend's excitement made Brianna envious. To be expecting a baby with the man you loved sounded like the best thing in the world.

Brianna asked the clerk to gift wrap her presents. Afterward, they stopped for a hamburger before parting ways. She was so anxious for the next day that she didn't sleep very well.

Saturday turned out to be an especially busy day at the saddlery. At twelve thirty Brianna told her uncle she was leaving. He smiled and told her to have a great time. No more talks like the one they'd had Tuesday night.

After freshening up, she walked out to the truck with her gifts, aware of her heart thudding out of control. Under her parka she wore a pair of white jeans and a new, dark blue crepe blouse that buttoned up in front with a roll collar and pockets. The cuffed sleeves fastened below the elbow. She wanted to look beautiful for Eli.

Though it was close to freezing, no storms had been forecasted for the next three days. The sun was out today and the main highway was free of snow. Brianna turned in to the Clayton ranch and drove past the main house until she reached Eli's. His mother's Land Rover was parked in front, but there was no sign of his truck.

Surprised, she got out of her uncle's truck with the gifts and walked to the front porch. Before she had a chance to ring the bell, the door opened.

"Mrs. Clayton—"

"Hello, Brianna. I saw you pull up. Please come in."

She entered the house and closed the door behind her. "Is Libby sick again?"

"No, no. Luke, one of the stockmen, had a heart attack while they were all working this morning. He has no family in Montana so Eli drove him to the hospital and is staying with him until the foreman can get there to be with him. I'm sure Eli will be back as soon as he can."

"Of course. The poor man. I hope he got him there in time."

"We're all praying for that. As for Libby, she's had lunch and is taking her nap right now. Give me your parka." Brianna removed it so Eli's mother could hang it in the hall closet. "Why don't we go sit down in the living room?"

"Thank you."

"Have you had lunch?" Mrs. Clayton asked.

"Not yet, but I'm not hungry."

"Coffee, then?"

"No, thank you. I'll wait for Eli. If he doesn't get back soon, I'll fix myself something. Please feel free to go if you want."

"Well, if you're sure…"

Brianna nodded. "I'll stay here with Libby for as long as I'm needed. When she wakes up, I have a few things to give her."

Eli's mother looked at the gifts she'd put on the couch. "How exciting!"

"I hope she'll like them."

"That's very sweet of you."

Brianna smiled. "It's easy to want to spoil that child."

"Tell me about it." The older woman laughed.

"Eli has told me several times how grateful he is for you and how bad he feels you've had to do so much for him and Libby. Let me take over now so you can do whatever you want for the rest of the day."

"Solana and I do need to go grocery shopping..."

"Then go, enjoy and don't worry about us."

Mrs. Clayton walked out to the foyer and pulled her parka from the hall closet. After putting it on, she turned to Brianna. "I know my granddaughter is in the best of hands with you. She has said your name no fewer than a dozen times since I came over to help."

Those words thrilled Brianna. "I can't wait to play with her."

Eli's mother eyed her for a moment. "My son told me what a great support you were when Libby was in the hospital."

"When I heard she had croup, I wanted to be there."

"Eli is very lucky to know you." She reached in her purse and pulled out a business card for the gem shop. "This has my cell phone number on it if you need me for any reason."

Brianna took it from her. "Thank you so much."

"I'll be back home in an hour. In the meantime, Libby has a sippy cup if you want to give her milk. Eli also has crackers and bananas on hand should you decide to put her in the high chair for a snack. There's baby food on the shelf."

"I'm sure he has everything. Libby and I will be fine."

"I have no doubt of it."

"Oh, and by the way, if I haven't told you before,

my aunt adores her ring. I believe it has made her fall in love with my uncle all over again."

"How lovely," she said and smiled warmly. "I'll talk to you soon."

Brianna watched her walk to her Land Rover and drive off, then she went down the hallway to check on Libby and discovered the little monkey was awake. Through the gap in the doorway, she saw the toddler sitting up in her crib, playing with her polar bear. Her brown hair was in tangles, melting Brianna's heart.

Libby saw her and immediately got to her feet, clinging to the crib railing. "Bree—"

"Good afternoon, darling." She rushed over and picked her up. Those little arms were surprisingly strong as they wrapped around her neck. She gave Brianna a kiss on the cheek.

"Shall we change your diaper and put on one of your outfits?" She gave her kisses on both cheeks. "Then I have some treats for you."

Once she'd decked her out in a little brown-and-yellow cowboy outfit, she reached for Libby's hair brush and book from the dresser and carried her into the living room. To Brianna's delight, Eli's daughter spotted the brightly colored gifts on the couch at once and squirmed to get down.

"So, you love presents just like everyone else! Of course you do. Here you go." She handed her the box of moons. Libby sat down and started to tear the paper away. Brianna got down on her knees to watch and help her lift off the lid.

The moons spilled onto the carpet. She grabbed the yellow one.

Brianna tapped it. "Moon. Moon. See? These are all moons." She laid them out in a line. To help her understand, she put the *Goodnight Moon* book on the floor and opened it to the picture of the moon.

The little girl studied it and then looked at the moons before she reached for the white one and gazed up at Brianna. She was smart, just like her daddy. "Moo."

"Moon. That's right."

"Moo."

The *n* would have to come later. Libby picked out the dark blue half moon. "That is a moon, too," Brianna said. "Moon."

But Libby wasn't as interested in the half-moons. She started playing with the six pancake-like moons. Brianna took advantage of the moment to brush Libby's brown hair into curls. She really was a beautiful child.

The sound of the doorbell startled Brianna, but Libby was riveted with her new toy.

Who could it be?

Brianna put the brush down and got to her feet. She walked to the entrance and said, "Who is it?"

"Tessa Clayton. I'm here to see my daughter."

What?

Brianna's body went hot and then cold before she opened the door. Immediately she recognized the attractive woman standing there from the pictures Eli had placed around the nursery. Libby was the spitting image of her.

"Please. Come in."

"Thank you." She stepped inside the entrance hall.

"H-have you made arrangements with Mr. Clayton?" Brianna's voice faltered.

"No. He couldn't be reached, but I assure you I'm Libby's mother. Are you Sarah, her nanny?"

Good Heavens. "No. My name is Brianna Frost. I'm watching Libby right now." At this point Libby toddled into the foyer with a moon in both hands. Brianna bit her lip. "Perhaps you should check with Mrs. Clayton first?"

"I stopped at the ranch house, but no one was there."

Brianna couldn't believe this was happening. "Have you tried to reach Eli?"

"Not yet. I just want to see her. Eli came to see me a week ago and told me I could visit my daughter any time."

Think, Brianna. This is what Eli had been wanting all along. He'd gone to Thompson Falls to try one last time to work things out with his ex-wife. Now that she'd come all this way to see her little girl, who was Brianna to tell her she couldn't?

She pulled Libby into her arms. "Come in the living room, Mrs. Clayton."

Libby hid her head in Brianna's neck. This was a situation she couldn't have anticipated in a million years. She thought how strange it must be for Libby's mother to come back to this house where she'd lived with Eli, where she'd planned their baby's nursery. And now Brianna was inviting *her* in.

She carried Libby all the way in and set her down on the floor by her new toys, hoping they would distract her. Brianna sat down next to her. Tessa perched on the end of the couch by the two of them. She, too, was wearing jeans with a V-necked kelly green sweater.

Floundering for words, Brianna said, "I just brought her this present because she loves the book *Goodnight Moon*. It's her favorite."

"Eli and I bought it right before she was born."

Shock number two.

"If you'd like to hand her that unopened gift, she'll probably behave more naturally."

Tessa reached for it and handed it to her daughter. "Would you like to open this, Libby?"

At first Brianna didn't think Libby would accept it, but curiosity won her over. Libby started pulling the paper off to reveal the coloring book of moons. She opened the pages and pointed at the various moon faces. Brianna looked up at Tessa. In a low voice she said, "Why don't you get on the floor, too, and open the box of crayons for her? Show her what to do."

Tessa slid off the couch and moved down on the carpet. Brianna fought to control her breathing while Tessa opened the crayon box and watched to see what would happen.

Tessa pulled out a red crayon and started coloring one of the faces in the opened book. "Do you want to color, too?" she asked Libby, handing her the box.

Her little girl picked out the blue crayon, the same shade as one of the toy moons. The two of them sat there and colored. "That's a beautiful blue moon," she told her daughter.

Brianna's eyes blurred to see mother and daughter doing a project together. Since Libby's birth, this was what Eli had been wanting and praying for. "I'll be right back," she whispered. Reaching for her purse, Brianna disappeared from the living room and hurried through the house to the bathroom. She dug inside her bag for Eli's mother's business card and called her.

"Mrs. Clayton? This is urgent. Can you come to the house right now? Just walk in."

The older woman didn't ask any questions. She said she'd be right there. Brianna rejoined Tessa and Libby in the living room. The two of them were coloring more pages and seemed to be having a good time. A minute later, Eli's mother walked through the door into the living room. She hadn't even paused to put on her parka.

Brianna saw the shock on the older woman's face. And the love... "Tessa," she cried softly.

The woman's brown head lifted. "Mom Clayton?" There was affection in her voice.

"Don't get up, honey. Stay right there with Libby."

Brianna knew what this moment meant to the older woman, who'd been praying for this miracle, too.

But Libby had heard her grandmother's voice and got to her feet to show her the crayon she'd been using. "Have you been coloring?"

"Moo," she said with great emotion.

"Ah." She walked over and hunkered down beside her granddaughter. "I can see the moon."

The three of them coloring together was a sight Brianna would never forget. If Eli could see this right now... Maybe he could. She pulled out her phone and took some pictures to show him.

While they were all engaged, Brianna tiptoed over to the foyer and got her parka out of the closet. This was one of those exits that didn't need to be explained. Instead of leaving by the front door, she hurried through the kitchen to the back porch. She had to traipse through six inches of snow, but it was worth it not to be detected.

After reaching her truck, Brianna prayed she wouldn't see Eli on her way out to the highway. Instead of turning left toward Stevensville, she made a right and drove the twenty-mile loop back to her uncle's house.

The miracle had happened.

Brianna didn't question what she did next. While en route, she stopped long enough to make a reservation for a flight to California that night. She followed that up with a call to her brother. When she told him she was coming home and would explain later, he said he'd meet her at the airport in Sacramento.

Her aunt and uncle weren't home when she arrived at the house. They'd thought she'd be gone until late, so maybe it was better this way. She called a taxi and made arrangements to be picked up ASAP for the trip to the Missoula airport. Then she hurriedly packed.

Before the taxi arrived, she wrote a letter for her family to read when they got home.

Later on in the year she'd fly back to gather all her belongings. For the time being, she just needed to leave Montana. When Eli walked into his house, his whole world was going to change. Brianna didn't want to be there.

Tessa had obviously experienced a huge breakthrough. It appeared Eli's visit the week before had done something that no therapy could accomplish. He didn't need outside stress while he dealt with the fact that his ex-wife had come to see their daughter.

Brianna didn't want to jump to any conclusions yet. All she knew was that, after a whole year, Tessa had made an appearance. Who knew what would happen when he found her in their house, wanting to be with Libby? If all went well, their little girl would be getting her mother back.

Maybe Tessa's feelings for Eli had been rekindled by seeing him face-to-face, too. Nothing was impossible, but the thought of those two getting back together hurt more than anything. It was too painful for her to watch it happen.

ELI LEFT THE hospital and had just climbed into his truck when his mother called. He clicked on his cell phone. "Mom? Luke is going to be all right. They have to do tests, but after a few days they'll go in to repair a valve in his heart. Luis is with him until his girlfriend gets there, so I'm coming home right now."

"Well, that's great news, Eli. I'm relieved to hear

you got him to the hospital in time. Now, there's something I've got to tell you. Tessa showed up at your house out of the blue this afternoon to see Libby."

He reeled. "She *what?*"

"I guess she decided to surprise you, too."

"With Brianna there?"

"Yes. Brianna let her in and called me to come over. While I was occupied with Tessa and Libby, Brianna left your house without telling me. I'm sure she went back to her aunt and uncle's because she knew how important this unexpected visit was."

His hand almost crushed the phone. He closed his eyes tightly. "Where is Tessa?"

"Carl and Diane drove her here. The three of them are staying at the Bitterroot Lodge in town. She just left the house and hopes to talk to you when you're free this evening. I took Libby home with me and will keep her overnight. Tessa's waiting for you to call her."

This was unbelievable.

But someone else was waiting for him, too. Someone who'd become so important to him that he needed to talk to her before he did anything else.

"What would I do without you, Mom? I'll be in touch soon."

He started the engine and headed straight for the Frost home. As he turned into the driveway, he had to put on his brakes. A taxi was getting ready to back out. That outfit ran a service to the Missoula airport.

Realizing what it meant, a pit formed in his gut.

He left his truck blocking the driveway and got out. The driver honked, but Eli kept moving toward the taxi and opened the back door.

"Eli—" Brianna looked shaken.

"Yes. Where do you think you're going?"

"It's clear Tessa is back and wants to be a part of your and Libby's lives. Your world changed today. So did mine. You three deserve to be together." Her voice shook.

"Well, this is one trip you're not going to take." He went around to the driver and handed him forty dollars, half the amount to get her to the airport. "Thanks for coming, but she's changed her mind. I'll grab her luggage."

Eli opened the other rear door and pulled out her suitcase, and then he returned to where she was sitting. "Come and get in my truck so the man can back out. I'm not taking no for an answer."

He'd put her in a bad position, but he didn't care. She got out without making a scene and followed him to his truck. After helping her inside and putting her suitcase on the rear seat, he got behind the wheel and moved so the taxi could leave.

"Tessa and her parents drove here from Thompson Falls and are staying at the Bitterroot Lodge. I have to stop by and see them, and then you and I are going to have a long talk."

"Wait, Eli—if we're going to leave, I need to take my luggage back to my bedroom and get the letter I left for my aunt and uncle."

He groaned. She'd covered all her bases in such

a big hurry that it astounded him he'd been able to catch her before she'd managed to sneak away. Eli took a swift breath and drove back into the driveway. He pulled the suitcase out and carried it to the door for her. Then he waited in the truck until she came out again.

"I'm going to have to cancel my flight and call my brother."

"You can do that while we're on our way over to the lodge. When we get there, we'll get something to eat in the coffee shop and I'll give their room a call."

After a silence she asked, "Have you seen her?"

"Not yet. As soon as Luis showed up at the hospital to be with Luke, I was able to leave. Mom phoned and explained what had gone on while I wasn't home. The second she told me you had disappeared, I drove straight here from the hospital. Another fifteen seconds and I would have been too late."

"You have to understand—" she began, but he didn't let her finish.

"I do. But you have to understand something, too. For now let's just take care of first things first, and then we'll talk. Agreed?"

"Yes," she whispered.

"As you know, one of our hands had a heart attack today. When I heard you'd slipped away from my house without saying good-bye, I almost had one myself. I recall a certain conversation where you promised me you'd give me fair warning."

She stirred restlessly. "All the rules changed this afternoon."

"They certainly did."

By the time he'd pulled into the parking lot of the lodge, she'd cancelled her flight and had left a message on her brother's voice mail.

In the coffee shop, the hostess showed them to a table and gave them menus before walking away. Eli didn't need to look at one. "If you'll order me steak and eggs and plenty of coffee, I'll be back soon."

"Eli?" she said as he stood up.

"What is it?"

Her heart was in those blue eyes that stared at him with such concern. "This *is* what you wanted."

"For Libby to have her mother's love—yes, it's what I've wanted. But not for you to disappear."

"I believe it's for the best."

"Not for me it isn't." Her unselfishness was a rare trait that meant more to him than she would ever know. He shook his head before leaning over to kiss her mouth. "I'll be right back."

The taste of her lips lingered on his as he walked to the front desk and called Tessa's room on the house phone.

"Eli?" It was Carl's voice.

"Yes. I'm at the front desk, but I've just come from the hospital and need to get home soon. If you're staying the night, I'd like to have a proper visit with all of you first thing in the morning at my house. We'll have breakfast with Libby. But if you have to leave tonight, I can come up to your room now."

"No, no. Tomorrow will be perfect. We all need sleep."

He could only imagine. "How did Tessa react to being with Libby?"

"She can't stop talking about how wonderful her baby is."

Eli's throat thickened. "Thank God." Major, major progress had been made.

"Bless you for coming to see her last week," Carl said with tears in his voice.

"See you in the morning," Eli told him.

He hung up, dazed by the events that had happened throughout the day. Brianna's plea not to give up on his wife had resulted in a turnaround of earthshaking proportions. This could potentially be the start of Libby's relationship with her mother.

When he returned to the coffee shop, he found Brianna eating an omelet and sipping on coffee. She looked up as he slid into the booth. Her searching eyes asked all the questions he attempted to answer.

"Tessa and her parents will be at my house in the morning to have breakfast with Libby. After they leave, you and I will enjoy the day we should have had today." He sat down to eat his meal.

"Don't worry about tomorrow because of what happened today." Brianna reached in her purse for her phone. "I want to show you something." She clicked on her photo gallery and found the pictures she'd taken earlier. "Take a look at these."

Eli took the phone from her. She saw him magnify the pictures. When he looked up, his eyes had gone suspiciously bright.

"I bought crayons and a coloring book of moon

faces for Libby. I had Tessa give them to Libby after she arrived. At that point, I called your mother and she came over. Pretty soon the three of them were on the floor, coloring away. I couldn't resist taking some photos so you could see for yourself."

She heard his sharp intake of breath. "You're incredible, Brianna." He grasped her hand across the table. "I'm so indebted to you for turning their first meeting into something wonderful. I'm at a loss for words."

"It all happened very naturally. Perhaps because of the pictures of Tessa around Libby's room and your recent trip to go see her, Libby didn't act at all strange around her. But maybe that's because they were together for the first month of her life."

"Maybe. Whatever the reason, I know the encounter went well or Tessa wouldn't have wanted to stay over until tomorrow in order to talk to me."

Honesty forced Brianna to explain the rest. "But the truth is I almost didn't let her in, Eli."

"That doesn't matter." He gave her hand a squeeze before letting go. "She took us all by surprise. I did the same thing to her by showing up at her door unannounced. I'm sorry it put you in an awkward position."

"It's all right. At first she thought I had to be Sarah."

"What did you tell her?"

"That I was a friend looking after Libby. While they were all busy coloring, I decided the best thing to do was leave the three of them alone. I knew that without my presence, Tessa and your mother would be able to talk more freely until you got there."

He wiped his mouth with a napkin. "And, knowing how your mind works, I guess you decided to get as far away as you could in order to make it possible for me and Libby to reunite with Tessa and for us to get remarried. That's what you told your aunt and uncle in that letter you didn't want me to see, right? Don't bother to deny it."

She eyed him directly. "I won't."

Since she'd finished eating, Eli put some bills on the table and got to his feet. "Let's go."

Once more he walked her out to the truck where they could talk in total privacy. "Before I drive you home, let me make one thing clear. I'm not the same man I was a year ago. Even if I hadn't met you, I don't have the kinds of feelings for Tessa I once had. They're dead and can't be resurrected."

"How can you be so sure?"

"Let me ask you a question. When you were in your previous relationships and decided to break up with those guys, how could you be so sure you were making the right decision?"

It took her a while. "Though I felt love for them in different ways, I knew I wasn't *in* love with them."

"And you never wanted them back."

"No."

"I don't want to get back with Tessa and am positive she doesn't want to get back with me. Only time will tell if she wants a full relationship with Libby and we work out visitation."

He could hear her mind working.

"There's a question I want to ask you, Eli, but if you can't, or don't want to, answer it, that's fine."

"Put that way, I'm going to have to. Otherwise it will lurk in your mind and fester."

She let out a sad laugh. "This is about something your father told my uncle right before you got married."

"What did he say?"

"He was worried that you were rushing into your marriage."

Eli remembered that conversation very well. "And?" He knew there was an *and*.

"There's nothing else."

He didn't believe her.

Brianna shifted in the seat. "Why do you think your father said it?"

"Because he was right. We did get married too fast. No doubt your uncle passed on that bit of insight to you because he's afraid I'm getting ahead of myself again."

"I shouldn't have said anything," she murmured.

"I'm glad you did. No secrets between us, remember? So here's another truth. Tessa wanted to get married right away, but I didn't. I wished we'd waited another year so I could have earned more money on the circuit before working on the ranch again."

"Obviously she was in love and couldn't bear to wait."

He let out a sigh. "She made it clear that if we put it off, she wouldn't be around for me in a year's time.

Though I didn't know it then, I now realize that she was in love with the idea of love and it made her impatient to get married. We had a serious problem because I wanted to stay on the circuit and get married a year later. That upset her and we didn't see each other for a month. While I was away at another rodeo, I learned from Wymon that she'd come down with the flu and was really sick. I went to see her and before I left the house, we set a date."

Brianna leaned closer. "Did your father know all that history?"

"No. That was my business. Toly always confided in Dad about everything. My older brothers did, too, from time to time, but I guess I was different in that regard."

"So because you kept quiet about the situation with Tessa, *that's* why my uncle called you complicated."

"Yes. Thank you for providing the other part of the *and*. I've been waiting to hear what you were holding back." Eli pulled her toward him. "Thank you for being so completely you. I adore you, Brianna," he cried softly and drew her into his arms, devouring her until some people got in the car parked next to them.

A male voice said, "Those two ought to get a room." The female voice laughed, breaking the trance that held them both.

Eli released the woman who'd become his whole world. "I'm going to get you home and we'll start over again tomorrow after Tessa and her family leave for Thompson Falls. I'll come by as soon as I can. Please tell me you'll be free. That's the only way I'm going to make it through tonight's separation."

"I'll be free, but I'll understand if something unavoidable comes up."

"It won't." Eli meant it and gave her a fierce kiss before letting her move to her side of the truck.

Chapter Eight

After being kissed breathless outside on the porch, Brianna entered the house on unsteady legs. Her aunt and uncle were watching TV. Taffy lay in front of the fire. Brianna had hoped to go straight to her bedroom without being noticed, but no such luck. The dog got up and wandered over to her.

The TV went off. "Hi, honey. Did you have a good time with Libby and Eli?"

She removed her parka and sank down on one of the chairs. "You won't believe all the things that happened today, Aunt Joanne."

"Tell us. It has to be better than TV was tonight," her uncle teased.

"Well, for starters, Mrs. Clayton was at the house when I got there because one of the stockmen at the ranch had a heart attack and Eli had taken him to the hospital."

"Oh, no. That's terrible."

"I know. And then, after his mother left, I was playing with Libby when a surprise visitor showed up at the door."

"Who?"

"Tessa Clayton, Eli's ex-wife. Out of the blue, she decided to come see her daughter."

Both her aunt and uncle got to their feet, looking incredulous.

"I'm sure I looked just like you when I answered the door. At first she thought I was the nanny. I invited her in and we went into the living room where Libby had been playing with some toys I'd given her. I put Libby back down and Tessa joined her on the floor."

"And Libby was okay?" her aunt asked.

"Completely. I phoned Eli's mother to come over, and after she arrived, all three of them started coloring on the floor together. I took a picture. When you see it, you'll understand why my first instinct was to leave Eli's house right away. And that's only the beginning of what happened."

"Take your time. We've got all night," her uncle said.

Shock marred Uncle Clark's and Aunt Diane's features as Brianna told them how she'd almost flown to California, only to have Eli put a stop to that. "Tessa and her family are staying at the Bitterroot Lodge until tomorrow. They've arranged to go over to Eli's in the morning, but he wants to spend the rest of the day with me after they go back."

"Oh, honey." Her aunt put an arm around her. "I can't even imagine how you must be feeling right now."

"It's kind of like waking up from a strange dream. It's hard to tell what's real right now."

Her uncle studied her with concern. "I hope you told him you had other plans for tomorrow."

It could easily have been her father speaking. For once her aunt didn't interject. "Uncle Clark... I know what you're thinking, but Eli and I had a long talk tonight and I understand why his father said what he did about him not being ready for marriage. It's not what you think, but, to be honest, I'm exhausted and I'll tell you the rest in the morning."

She gave them each a hug. "Thank you both for being so wonderful to me. I'm very lucky you're my family. Good night."

Brianna hurried to her room, needing to process everything that had happened now that Eli's arms weren't around her. When he was kissing her, she couldn't think straight. Not two minutes after she'd climbed into bed and pulled the covers over her, her phone rang. She reached for it on the bedside table and saw the caller ID.

"*Eli—*"

"Thank you for answering. I couldn't go to bed without hearing your voice." She could relate. "Do your aunt and uncle know what happened today?"

"Yes."

"Everything?"

"Yes."

"Then I guess they don't want you spending the day with me tomorrow."

"It's my decision," she told him. "They would

never interfere." Brianna rolled on her other side. "Is Libby at your mom's?"

"No. Mom stayed with her until I got here."

"She's a saint."

"Interestingly enough, that's what she said about you today. I saw the painted moons you gave Libby. Your gifts were such a big hit. Mom said Libby went to sleep holding the big, dark blue moon. I found it in the crib and put it in the box with the others. We're going to have a lot of fun with those. How do I begin to thank you for everything?"

"Toys and children belong together."

"I'm talking about the way you handled the situation with my ex-wife. I don't know another woman who would have done what you did to help Tessa and Libby feel secure at the same time."

"She wanted to see her daughter."

"If they end up having a relationship, it will be because of you."

"That's not true."

"We'll argue about it later. Mom said the two of them seemed so comfortable with each other. That's *your* doing, Brianna. You urged me not to give up. If I hadn't gone to Thompson Falls last week, I'm certain this never would have happened." His voice had grown husky.

Her eyes teared up. "They belong together. Anyone could see that."

"I know another thing beyond any doubt. *We* belong together." She prayed he meant it. "I'll see you tomorrow. Sweet dreams."

Brianna hung up, clasping the phone to her heart. *I love you, Eli Clayton. I love you.*

"COME ON, SWEETIE. Now that we've had breakfast, let's go get some toys." Eli lifted Libby out of the high chair and nodded to Tessa to follow him. They left her parents at the kitchen table and headed for the nursery.

After he put his daughter on the Hello Kitty area rug, he found the little basket of blocks and dumped them on the floor in front of her. "Do you want to show your mommy how to build a castle?"

Tessa got down on the floor with her and the three of them started working together. This was his first chance to talk to his ex-wife alone. "I'm so glad you came, Tessa. How does it feel to be with her?"

"It means everything to me. After I saw her in your arms last weekend, something seemed to snap inside of me. Our daughter just looked so beautiful... and so familiar, too."

"How do you mean?"

"Well, I can see both our families in her. That face spoke to my heart. For the first time in a year I felt alive. After you left, I called the doctor. We talked about what had happened to me. He suggested that I come here this weekend and see if I felt the same way. I knew my feelings wouldn't have changed because her image has haunted me all week."

He wasn't thrilled that she hadn't phoned him first to let him know her plans. She had put Brianna in a terrible position, but there was nothing anyone could do about it now. Eli watched tears roll down Tessa's cheeks as she placed another block on top of the one Libby had just set down.

"I know I've been very sick and you have every right to tell me to stay away for good."

"You're her mother, Tessa, and she needs you. If you want to see her, we can work it out, easy. It's up to you."

She put a hand to her mouth. "You're such a good man. I don't deserve you."

"That isn't an issue. Libby's the light of my life. For her to be truly happy she needs both her parents. Agreed?"

Tessa nodded. "You didn't want to get married as soon as I did. Then, after I got sick, I pushed you away. I thought I didn't want to be married anymore and I'm so sorry about that, but I do want to take care of our daughter."

"Then we'll work it out. Talk to your doctor and ask him what he suggests. The next time you come, I'll introduce you to Sarah. We can take turns driving back and forth from Thompson Falls."

Fear entered her eyes. "Do you think it's too late for her to accept me?"

"She's playing blocks with you. That should tell you everything you want to know."

Tessa smiled. "She is, and she's doing a great job, too." She kissed her daughter's head.

They kept playing for a little while and then Libby suddenly got up. "Moo." She pointed to the box on the dresser. Eli got it for her. They sat down again and he removed the lid.

"What are these?" Tessa asked her. Eli's daughter emptied the box and began sorting the moons. "These are so cute. Where did you get them, Eli?"

"You met Brianna yesterday, right? She bought them for Libby."

"Bree—" his daughter said unexpectedly.

Tessa glanced at him. "When we met yesterday, she told me she was a friend."

"She's done business with Mom at the gem shop. You remember Frosts' Western Saddlery in town? Brianna works there for her uncle and helped him pick out a stone to give her aunt for their anniversary. She met Libby and played with her while mom mounted the stone for him. I started seeing her after that."

He knew Tessa was wrapping her mind around what he'd just told her and decided this was a good time to leave the nursery. "Tell you what. I'm going to slip into the living room for a few minutes. Let's see how you two get along alone."

"I don't know…"

"I think you'll be fine, but if you don't feel comfortable yet, that's all right."

"I'd rather you stayed."

It was hard to say no to Tessa. It always had been.

Eli tousled Libby's curls. "Do you want to show Mommy your push toy? It's over there in the corner."

Libby knew the word *push* and got up to find it. Pretty soon she was rolling the helicopter around the room while Tessa clapped and made excited sounds.

All of a sudden Tessa got on her hands and knees and started chasing Libby. "I'm going to get you!" she said.

His daughter giggled and started running faster. Eli could hardly breathe. A week ago he couldn't have imagined this happening.

"Well, well. What's going on in here?" Carl and Diane had come into the nursery to see what all the excitement was about. Libby stopped running and came over to hug Eli.

Tessa rolled over on her back and smiled up at them. It was great to see her look that happy again. "Libby and I have been playing, but I think she's had enough for now." She got to her feet and turned to Eli. "We should go back, but I'll call you after I've talked to my doctor."

"Sounds good," Eli said and got to his feet. He carried Libby to the front of house. Tessa and her parents pulled on their parkas and he walked them to the front door.

"Bye, Libby," they all said. Tessa looked at their daughter with longing before kissing her good-bye.

Though Libby clutched him tightly, she did say bye. "Bye, Mommy," he encouraged his daughter to say, but she didn't.

When they'd left, he carried her back to the nursery and walked over to the larger picture of Tessa. "Mommy," he said the word several times, pointing to the photo. "Can you say *Mommy*?"

He waited, but she started to squirm and said, "Moo."

Eli smiled to himself. This was the best beginning he could have hoped for. He had to remember the old adage that Rome wasn't built in a day. Now it was time to phone Brianna. He checked his watch. It was noon. After putting Libby on the floor, he pulled out his cell phone.

Brianna answered on the second ring. "Hi!"

Just hearing her voice excited him. "Libby and I are on our way over to get you. Have you eaten lunch?"

"Not yet."

"Good. We'll stop somewhere and get hamburgers. Libby likes fries and soft ice cream."

"So do I. How fun."

"I thought after that maybe we could take a walk in the Lee Metcalf National Wildlife Refuge, and then bring her home for a nap."

"Perfect. I'll be ready."

Eating lunch at the restaurant and pushing Libby around in her stroller at the nature preserve, Brianna felt as if they were a true family. Only two of the walks were free of snow, but they were able to see a fox, geese, some swans and an osprey. They both took pictures with their phones before heading back to the truck.

Libby appeared oblivious to the cold, all bundled up in her snowsuit. The little girl had worked her way into Brianna's heart. As for her father...

When they got back to Eli's house, they entertained Libby until Eli put her down for a nap. Then he pulled Brianna into the living room. He threw some cushions down on the floor and they lay by the fire he'd made.

"This is the kind of day I'd planned for yesterday." He kissed the tips of her fingers.

She was dying to know his thoughts. "Tell me how things went with Tessa this morning," she said.

"Better than I could have hoped for," he admitted. "She said my visit last week broke down some barrier in her mind. She wants to be a mother after all."

Brianna's eyes filled with tears. "You must be overjoyed."

"I am. I told her to talk to her doctor and that we'd work things out as far as visitation and things go."

"I'm sure you have concerns."

He nodded. "What if this change of heart doesn't last and she decides she doesn't want to be a mom to Libby after all? For Libby to get to know her mother and then be rejected is too painful to think about, but it's something I have to consider."

"Maybe you should talk to her doctor about this."

His eyes studied her for a long moment. "That's exactly what I'm going to do with Tessa's permission. How did you get to be so wise?"

"TV."

"*Brianna*—" He pulled her close and started kissing her. She'd been aching for him.

"I want you," he whispered. "You have no idea how beautiful you are and how much I need you."

"I feel the same way," she confessed. The floodgates had been released. To be able to explore her feelings, knowing one of Eli's greatest concerns might be getting resolved, allowed her to open up to him completely. She couldn't get enough of him. No kiss was long enough or deep enough. Soon she found herself on top of him, their legs entwined. She could kiss every part of his ruggedly handsome face and hard, sinewy body. He was such a gorgeous man.

"Do you love me?" he demanded urgently after rolling them over so he could look down into her eyes.

"Oh, Eli—you *know* I do. I think I've loved you from the first time I saw you."

He kissed the corners of her mouth. "I've already told you I'm in love with you. I want to marry you as soon as possible."

Her breath caught. She cried his name, but he stifled any other sounds with a passion that swept her away to a place where she couldn't deny him anything. The words rang in her ears.

Eli wanted to *marry* her.

Those words brought joy to every last atom in her body. It was just as her mother had said she would feel when she met the right man.

When he finally came up for air, he said, "Don't tell me it's too soon to talk about becoming my wife. We both know our feelings run so deep there can be no doubt we're meant to be together, but I'm aware you might have reservations about becoming a stepmom."

She shook her head. "I already love Libby."

He caught her face between his hands. "Loving her and being a mother to her day and night for the rest of our lives are two different things. I'm positive that when you thought about getting married one day, it wasn't to a man who already had a child. It's too much to ask, yet I'm asking because I can't imagine my life without you."

Brianna sat all the way up, kissing his hand. "I love you so much it hurts. I want to be your wife. But now that Tessa has had a breakthrough, I'm wondering how she'll react to our getting married right away. Libby bonding with her mother is the most important thing."

"Our love is important, too, Brianna. I'll call her doctor first thing in the morning and tell him what's happened in case he doesn't already know. We'll go from there. But right now I want your answer. Will you marry me? We'll worry about the date later."

Brianna didn't have to think about it. "Yes! One hundred percent, yes!" She flung her arms around his neck. "You've made me the happiest woman alive, Eli Clayton."

ON MONDAY MORNING, while Eli was at the barn talking with Wymon about Luke's pending heart surgery, his phone rang. It was Dr. Rutherford.

He clicked on. "Thanks for getting right back to me. I know how busy you must be."

"I had messages from both you and Tessa today. The news about her visit to see Libby is remarkable, but because you're contemplating marriage to someone else, I need to talk to you about it right away."

Eli tensed. "I'm available to talk at five today. Will that work for you?"

"Yes, that's fine."

"Good. We'll talk then."

After hanging up, he rode with Wymon to the range where the vet was meeting them to finish the cattle vaccinations. When they stopped for lunch, Eli called Brianna, but he got her voice mail. Undoubtedly she was having a busy morning. He told her he'd be talking to Tessa's doctor after work and would phone her at dinnertime.

At five minutes to five he walked into his house and scooped Libby up in his arms. The call came on time and Sarah took over while he went in his bedroom and closed the door.

"Dr. Rutherford?"

"I listened to your message and here's my concern," the doctor said. "This woman you're planning to marry—how long have you known her?"

"Brianna and I met a month ago." Eli had been ready for that question. To the doctor's credit, he didn't respond with shock or derision.

"How bonded is she to Libby?"

"We've spent enough time together that Libby loves being with Brianna and cries when she has to leave the house. Last week she was in the hospital with croup. When Brianna walked in the room, Libby couldn't have shown more excitement or affection. She acts as comfortable around her as she does with my mother."

"That sounds promising for the three of you. As for Tessa, her phone call was a revelation. I understand their first meeting over the weekend went very well."

"It was amazing."

"Have you set a wedding date yet?"

"No, but it will be soon."

"Whatever visitation you work out with Tessa, the next time you see her, I suggest you tell her you're planning to get married and give her the date. Tessa will need to factor that information into her thinking. By her reaction, I'll know how stable she is.

"The whole goal is for Libby to have a relationship with her mother. So may I caution you to move carefully where Tessa is concerned?"

Eli heard him loud and clear. Brianna's uncle would add the punctuation points to that advice. "Libby's bond with her mother comes first, Dr. Rutherford." Brianna had said as much earlier.

"Good."

"Bill me for this phone meeting."

"Don't worry about it, and don't hesitate to call me again," the man said.

He hung up, not able to imagine what the doctor must be thinking about Eli having met another woman who he wanted to marry this fast. But this was Eli's life and no one else's. Knowing Brianna's feelings were just as strong helped him to act on his dream to make her his own.

Just as he was about to call her, his cell phone rang again. This time Tessa's name showed up on the caller ID.

He clicked on. "Tessa?"

"Hi!" There was a time when he would have given

anything to hear that voice. That had to be another lifetime ago. "I need to talk to you. Is that all right?"

"Of course." He sank down on the side of his bed. "What's on your mind?"

"I talked to the doctor today and told him I want to spend as much time with Libby as possible. Mom and I could drive to your house every day this week and spend time with her while you're at work, if that's okay. I know you have a nanny, but maybe we could work something out so I can be alone with her for part of the time? What do you think?"

Eli sucked in his breath. He could hear how nervous she was and wanted to reassure her. "I'm willing to work out anything so you can be with Libby. If you'd like to come every day, Sarah can disappear into her room while you're here. You and Libby can have the run of the rest of the house."

"You mean it?" Her cry rang right through the phone.

"Tessa, I always wanted you to be close to Libby. You're her mother."

"Thank you, Eli, from the bottom of my heart," his ex-wife said, her voice suffused with relief.

He got up and paced the floor for a minute. "There's one more thing we need to talk about before we hang up."

"Am I rushing you too much?"

"No. No, Tessa. This is about me, but it will affect you. As you know, I've been dating Brianna Frost since the last week of December. We're in love and want to get married in March." That was what he'd been planning in his mind. "When everything falls into place, it means there will be two women in Libby's life on a permanent basis."

Silence reigned. What she said next shook him to his foundation. "You must truly be in love to want to get married after only one month. I had to get sick in order for you to feel sorry enough for me to give in to my demands." She laughed as she said it, but he could tell the news upset her, and he couldn't blame her.

He frowned. "Don't compare the two situations."

"That's hard not to do. You weren't ready when we got married. This last year of therapy has taught me that I forced you into a marriage I wanted too much at the time and not for all the right reasons."

"I wouldn't have married you if I hadn't wanted to," he said.

"Even so, my guilt caught up to me after Libby was born. I was positive you hated me as much as I hated myself for preventing you from going out on the rodeo circuit another year. So I blocked you out. And I felt so worthless. I didn't believe I could be a good mother to Libby, so I blocked her out, too."

Eli marveled at the revelations pouring out of her. It was all starting to make sense.

"But when you brought her to the house two Saturdays ago, there she was, big as life and so beautiful. Eli—we have such a beautiful daughter."

He had to clear his throat. "Indeed we do."

"I want to prove that I can be a good mother. Tell me—is Brianna as in love with you as you are with her?"

"Yes." Thank Heaven. "We knew how deep we'd fallen for each other while Libby was recovering in the hospital."

"That's why I kept hearing Libby say the name *Bree* while she was playing with those toy moons. I had no idea another woman had become so important to you and her in such a short period of time."

"Just remember one thing, Tessa. She only has one mother. That's *you.*"

He heard her crying softly for a minute. "I can't believe you're giving me a second chance."

"That's because a part of me will always treasure the time we were married. Those memories will never be taken from me."

"I'll always love you, Eli, and our daughter means everything to me."

This was a conversation he'd never thought would happen. "Go ahead and make your plans to come tomorrow. I'll let Sarah know and we'll go from there."

"Mom and Dad are thrilled."

Yup. They would be. "We'll talk later, okay?"

The second he got off the phone with Tessa, he called Brianna and told her he was coming over. After they'd hung up, he went into the kitchen to talk to Sarah about what was going to happen for the rest of the week.

He got Libby prepared for bed and read her a story about an elephant, then took off for Stevensville. Tonight Tessa had sounded stable to Eli, even after he'd told her the news that he was in love again and planned to get married. As far as he was concerned, she appeared to have pulled a 180.

When he turned into the Frosts' driveway, Brianna came running outside and hopped into the truck. "You sounded so excited that I couldn't wait to hear your news."

Eli pulled her into his arms and kissed the daylights out of her. Nothing was holding him back now. "Not seeing you has made today feel like an eternity."

"Did you talk to Tessa's doctor?" she asked eagerly.

"Yes. There's so much to tell you that I don't know where to start, but I need to drive over to the hospital to see Luke before his operation in the morning. Then we'll have all night to talk. Don't you move one inch, all right?" He kissed her hungrily before backing out onto the street.

Two hours later, Eli drove Brianna back to her uncle's house. She'd been absorbing everything he told her. Though the news about Tessa was absolutely wonderful for Libby, it was the doctor's warning to Eli that made her a trifle anxious.

May I caution you to move carefully where Tessa is concerned?

That advice sank deep inside her.

Carefully could mean a lot of things. Tessa planned to drive here every day to see her daughter and be a mother to her. It seemed the most natural thing in the world now that Eli had explained what had gone on in Tessa's mind throughout their marriage. Time had been lost and she was eager to catch up.

Eli turned to her. "You're being quiet all of a sudden. Come over here, please."

"I don't dare. The second you touch me, I catch on fire."

"That's why we need to get married ASAP. Let's make it the first or second Saturday in March."

She moistened her lips nervously. "I want it more than anything, but I'm worried."

"Tell me why."

"You know as well as I do that Dr. Rutherford sent us both a message. Move carefully, he said. What he means is we need to give Tessa the best chance possible to bond with Libby. So far your little girl has already had to adapt to a nanny, then me, and now her mother. Since you need Sarah to help you, she has to stay in the picture, but *I* don't."

"Brianna—"

"Hear me out, Eli. Please." She took a swift breath. "Libby shouldn't have to be confused. A huge dose of her mother is exactly what she needs. The more they see each other, the sooner Libby will be comfortable staying overnight with her mother and grandparents in Thompson Falls. Once Tessa becomes a fixture in Libby's life, then Libby will be able to see me as the woman in *your* life."

His head reared back.

"You know I'm right. If I'm always over at your house, or you're at my place with Libby, it will prevent her from making that attachment to her mother. She needs to see you and Tessa together often so she makes the necessary association. If this plan is going to work, I can't be there."

It was a long time before he spoke. "So what are you saying?"

"I love you so much, Eli, but we need to separate in order to help Tessa and Libby make it as mother and daughter. I'm going to go back to California, hopefully tomorrow."

"If you do that, I'm going to lose you." He sounded so bleak that it wounded her.

"If our love isn't strong enough to survive this, then it isn't strong enough to endure over a lifetime."

A groan came out of him. "I couldn't take you being gone for more than a week."

"I think it'll need to be at least three weeks for this to work."

"Brianna—"

"I know. I can't bear the thought of it, either."

"What will you do?"

"I'll help on the farm. Be with my brother and his wife."

He sucked in his breath. "How do you think your aunt and uncle are going to feel about this?"

"When they know why I'm leaving, they'll tell me it's the right thing to do."

"That's what I'm afraid of."

"Eli, you and Tessa brought Libby into this world. This is Libby's chance to learn to love her mother the way you love yours. I know in my heart you would never deny her that opportunity. You need to concentrate on helping them bond without any other distractions. Your little Libby is already on her way to getting close to her mother."

"Your good sense is killing me."

"If I don't go, we won't be able to stay away from each other. Do you have a better idea?"

"I wish I did. Brianna—I don't know how I'm going to be able to let you go. I don't think I can." He kissed her with such intensity she went weak in his arms.

After he finally let her go, she looked up at him. "You do understand, don't you?"

His eyes bore into her soul. "To be separated from you now…"

"I don't like it, either. Please, Eli—never forget how much I love you. We'll talk every day until you feel it's time for me to come back." Brianna raised her mouth to his one more time before she tore herself from his strong arms and got out of the truck.

He levered himself from the cab to walk her to the front door. After another passionate embrace, she let herself inside. While she stood against the closed door, trembling, she heard him barrel out of the driveway.

Taffy limped into the foyer. Brianna petted her before making her way to the bedroom. Her aunt must have heard her come in and followed her.

"Honey? What's wrong?"

She wheeled around. Her pain had gone beyond tears. "I'm so sorry, but I have to go home tomorrow. Forgive me for leaving you in the lurch, but this is the only way."

"What do you mean?" her uncle said as he joined them.

"First of all, Eli has asked me to marry him and I've said yes."

"Oh, honey—you mean it?" Her aunt reached out to hug her, but her uncle stood there like a statue.

"The trouble is, when Eli spoke to Tessa's doctor today and told him about our plans to get married, he said to move carefully with her. Eli and I know what he meant. Tessa needs the chance to bond with Libby. The only way that's going to happen is for me to step out of the picture for a while."

"A very wise idea."

She'd expected her uncle to say that. "It seems Eli's surprise visit to their house last week proved to be the impetus that has brought Tessa around. She wants to be a mother to her daughter and will be coming here every day this week. The three of them need to work on this without me around. Do you understand?"

"You wonderful girl," her uncle said and wrapped his arms around her the way her father used to do.

No. She wasn't a wonderful girl. Dr. Rutherford was the one who'd pointed the way. If anyone was wonderful it was Eli, who was putting his daughter first, no matter how much he wanted Brianna with him. Talk about a man who matched these mountains...

ELI LEFT THE Clayton house with an idea he couldn't wait to present to Tessa. He had no intention of going longer than three weeks before he brought Brianna back from California.

En route to the ranch, he phoned his ex-wife, not caring how late it was.

"Eli?" Tessa sounded scared. "Have you changed your mind?"

"Of course not, but I have another idea. Why don't you ask your parents to drop you off here tomorrow and let you stay all week at the house? Sarah can go to Mom's and come over if she's needed."

"You'd let me do that? Be alone with her?" she almost squealed.

"Why not? If you're around Libby 24/7 for the whole week, you two should be able to bond more quickly. I'll drive you back home at the end of the week. Then we'll see if Libby wants to stay with you for a while. That is what you want, right?"

"You know it is." Her voice throbbed.

"Then let's do it. Call me when you get here and I'll come down from the range to help you get settled in."

If letting her live in his house would make this experiment work faster, then he could get the love of his life back sooner. Unfortunately, the fear that Tessa could suddenly develop inadequacy issues again haunted him. He didn't want to believe in another reversal, but Libby was her own little person and who knew what could happen.

There would probably be lots of anxious moments when Libby didn't turn to Tessa, which would prove difficult for her mom. Eli knew he was taking a risk and he would need to be patient. But it would all be worth it to marry Brianna once he knew Libby was secure in her mother's love.

Tomorrow he'd get up extra early and drive to the gem shop before work. He wanted another look at the dark blue sapphire, cut in the shape of a heart.

Blue sapphires with extremely high clarity were rare and very valuable. A three-carat stone of that quality was probably the most valuable of all the cut stones in his mother's collection.

Years ago she'd shown the stone to him and his brothers. She'd let them examine it with her handheld loupe. Their mom told them she was reserving it for just the right person. Most buyers wanted a round or princess cut. Not everyone wanted a heart-shaped stone. But whoever did would be getting a prize.

Not until he'd looked into Brianna's eyes for the first time and learned she was a Valentine baby did he think about that stone. For all he knew, his mother had sold it since then.

He would let himself inside the shop and open the safe to see if it was still there. Valentine's Day was coming up soon...

Chapter Nine

Brianna came out of the shower to hear the one o'clock newscast. It predicted that Valentine's Day would be the warmest day in Marysville so far this year. Seventy degrees with only a few tufts of clouds. After the twenties and low thirties of Montana, it was positively balmy in California.

Three long, agonizing weeks had passed since she'd flown back home. Brianna was surprised she'd lasted this long without seeing Eli. Her decision to leave had been the right one. Eli had come to realize it, too. His nightly phone calls let her know Libby and her mother were connecting. The wonderful news helped Brianna to survive.

Today was her birthday. She'd been waiting to hear from him since morning, but his call hadn't come. She finished dressing in the black dress she'd worn with him to the French restaurant in Missoula a month before. It felt like a hundred years since then. Doug and Carol were taking her to the Napa Valley for her birthday dinner celebration. If their parents were alive, they'd all be going.

One thing about living in Montana with her aunt and uncle was that Brianna had done her grieving away. Now that she was back home, it wasn't as hard as she'd thought it would be to live around the memories. The farm was thriving and Doug was so much happier than when she'd first left. They were able to laugh and reminisce without going to pieces.

But by the time they arrived at the Beaulieu Vineyard and walked around the gardens, she'd grown a little despondent. Why hadn't Eli called?

They were shown to their reserved table on the terrace and given menus. The terrace had a gorgeous view of the vineyard with a trellis roof overhead covered in red bougainvillea.

Once they were seated, Brianna eyed her brother critically. "You've worn a permanent smile on your face ever since we got in the car. What aren't you telling me?"

"It's your birthday, remember?"

"How could I forget? But you're acting like you've got a huge secret. Do you want me to open my present now? Is that what this is all about?" Carol averted her eyes, letting Brianna know something was going on. "If you don't tell me soon, I'm going to explode with curiosity."

"Well, we can't have that." Doug winked. "Okay, then. A few days ago Carol went to the doctor—"

"Get out of here!" Brianna cried out, knowing exactly what her brother meant.

"We're expecting in September but wanted to wait until you were here to tell you."

"Carol—" Brianna jumped up from her chair and ran around the table to hug both of them. "This is the best birthday present I've ever gotten. I'm going to be an aunt!"

Her joy was so all-consuming that she didn't realize someone was approaching their table. When she looked up, she almost passed out when she spotted Eli standing there. In his tan suit and white shirt, he was easily the most gorgeous male in the restaurant. Their gazes collided.

"Happy Birthday, Brianna."

In the periphery she saw the waiter make another place at the table, but she was so spellbound she couldn't move.

He hurried to her side and put an arm around her waist to support her. "I flew into Sacramento and rented a car. Your brother and I got acquainted over the phone and he told me where to find you," he whispered against her neck, kissing the soft, scented skin. "Come and sit down next to me."

"Eli—" She sagged against him. "I can't believe you're here."

"I've been planning this for two weeks. You have no idea how much I've looked forward to your birthday." His eyes worshipped her. "You're my valentine."

Somehow she made it to her seat with his help. He sat next to her and pulled a small, dark blue, velvet box from his suit pocket. "Open it. I don't want to wait."

Her heart thundered in her chest. With trembling hands, she opened the box and then gasped. Twilight had sneaked up on them. Light from the candle cen-terpiece lit up the facets of the large blue sapphire heart mounted in a white-gold setting.

"You already agreed to marry me. This makes it official." He took the ring out of the box and reached for her left hand, sliding it home on her ring finger.

The sapphire had to have come from the Clay-ton sapphire mine. She was thrilled out of her mind. "It's incredible."

"That's my heart. It's yours."

Tears ran down her cheeks. "This has to mean things are going well with Tessa and Libby. Oh, Eli—" Forgetting they had an audience, she threw her arms around his neck and clung to him.

"Brianna? The waiter is coming with our dinner."

Her brother's reminder forced her to let go of Eli. She knew her face was flushed.

"After we eat, we'll walk over to the other side of the restaurant where I can dance with my valentine," Eli whispered. "I've been dreaming about this mo-ment for so long."

She tried to behave, but it was close to impossible to be seated next to him and not climb on his lap and kiss him nonstop. Brianna had ached for him during their separation.

Doug and Carol congratulated the two of them, and Brianna told Eli they were expecting a baby. That led to talk about being a new father. She could tell her brother liked Eli a lot. But, oh, how happy she was when he asked her to dance and they were able to excuse themselves.

With his arm around her waist, he walked them through the restaurant to the dance floor, where a live band was playing. Dozens of red, pink and white heart-shaped balloons had been strung overhead. Eli pulled her against him and they moved as one to the music.

"I'm in Heaven right now," she murmured against his chest.

"You're not the only one. You look gorgeous tonight, by the way."

She was in an enchanted state when the lead singer announced that someone named Brianna was celebrating her birthday today. The band started to play "Happy Birthday" and everyone in the restaurant sang along.

"I can't believe you," she cried in surprise, hiding her face against Eli's shoulder.

"I gave him a tip before coming to join you."

Brianna finally lifted her head. "Eli? I'll never forget this night as long as I live."

"It's not over yet." He kissed her mouth and they danced until he said, "Let's go out to the rental car. I only have a half hour before I have to get back to the airport, and there are things we need to discuss in private."

What? "But you just got here—"

"I know. Wymon called the family together for some important ranching business we have to take care of tomorrow, so I have to get back to Missoula tonight. Even Toly is flying in from Reno after tonight's rodeo. Roce is going to meet us both at the airport and drive us to the ranch."

Eli said good-night to her brother and Carol, and they agreed to wait at the restaurant until Brianna got back. Then she and Eli headed out to the parking lot.

He slid behind the wheel of his rental car and pulled her into arms. They devoured each other before he finally pulled back and heaved a long sigh. "I have to go, Brianna," he said.

"I don't want you to leave. How am I going to let you go?" she asked.

He covered her face with kisses. "I want you to come back to Montana as soon as you can. Tomorrow if possible."

"That soon?" she cried with excitement. "Are you sure?"

"Positive. That ring is to remind you that we're going to be man and wife just as soon as we can find a date that works."

"Eli—" She tried to catch her breath. "While I can still think, tell me how it's really going with Tessa and Libby."

"The two of them are slowly making progress. I think letting Tessa sleep at the house for the first week was a good idea. We're all working on getting Libby to say *mama*, but it hasn't happened yet.

"Last week I drove Libby to Thompson Falls and stayed the night to see how she handled an overnight with Tessa and her family. She's been acquainted with her grandparents from the time she was born, but that night wasn't her best.

"They've set up a nursery, but she didn't want to be in there alone with Tessa unless she could see me. I ended up lying on the floor in a sleeping bag until she fell asleep. After breakfast we could tell she wasn't at ease, so Tessa went back with us and stayed all week.

"She's with her now and they seem very comfortable together at this point, but it's going to take time for Libby to get used to being away from the ranch with her."

"What about Sarah?"

"I'll continue paying her no matter what we work out. This week she's back home with her grandparents so Tessa and Libby can be completely alone in the house while I'm at work. Mom and Solana are nearby in case anything happens."

Brianna kissed his jaw. "I knew it wouldn't be easy, but it sounds like it's working."

"It is," he cried softly against her mouth. "That's why I want you back with me, Brianna—so we can make wedding plans. Call me after you've booked your flight, okay? I'll reimburse you after you're back."

She clung to him. The separation from him had only proved to her that, without Eli in her life, she couldn't imagine going on. Though people didn't die from a broken heart, they didn't fully live, either.

"I love you, Eli. I didn't know how much longer I could have lasted here without you."

"Don't you know I feel the same way? Soon we're going to be together forever."

Forever.

One more kiss and then she got out of the car and watched him drive away. All the way back to the patio where Doug and Carol were waiting, Brianna studied the spectacular engagement ring Eli had given her. To think he'd flown all this way just to give it to her on her birthday. The fact that he had to get right back for a family business meeting made it even more important to her.

ELI GLANCED AROUND the ranch house living room. It had been a while since the whole Clayton clan had assembled. Wymon had indicated this meeting was important. He wore an expectant look after they'd all found a place to sit.

"As you know, our father took out a lawsuit against the BLM three years ago because they started increasing our taxes for the acid mine drainage coming from our mine and polluting the water. It's happening to many metal mine owners throughout the West. The problem is that there are so many abandoned mines in the country, yet the BLM has to find the revenue to clean those up, too, so they get their money by gouging active mine owners.

"One solution proposed to Dad was to implement a water treatment plan at our mine, but it's terribly expensive. Worse, we will be sued if the water still didn't meet federal standards. In other words, under the Clean Water Act, even if we tried to clean up the drainage, we would be liable for any pollution that continued to flow from it.

"Dad got together with our attorneys to work out a

time frame with the BLM. But progress was slow and he feared a new tax would soon be levied against us. He tied up a lot of money to pay experts to come up with a different way to cut down on the contaminants, and we've been dealing with that problem ever since.

"Well, I'm here to tell you that our worries are over. The night before last, the lawyer told me the news that we've won the appeal. I'll read the history of the case for you.

"'Clark Fork is Montana's largest river and travels down from the Continental Divide. It threads its way between the Flint Creek, Sapphire and Garnet ranges that are filled with mines on its way to Missoula. In 1908, a flood washed tons of contaminated sediments from those mines into the river. Arsenic, copper, zinc, lead and cadmium contaminated millions of tons of sediment along 120 miles of the river's banks. The river's trout all but vanished.

"Montana is one of relatively few states that have active coal mining and one of still fewer allowed to use royalties from coal mines on non–coal mine reclamation. The state gets between three and four million dollars in Surface Mining Control and Reclamation Act royalties per year to deal with thousands of contaminated sites, not nearly enough to help its lands recover from over a century of mining.

"There are more environmental problems associated with abandoned mine lands than there will ever be funding to take care of them. If there was a federal royalty for the metal-mining industry, there could be a consistent source of funding revenue. Unlike oil, gas and coal industries, the metal-mining industry does not have to pay royalties to the federal government. This is due to the 1872 Mining Law, which hasn't been updated since it was first passed in an attempt to encourage the settlement of the West.

"In the case of the Sapphire Ranch versus the BLM, the Clayton Sapphire Mine is still active and taxes were levied against the mine because of the drainage coming from it. Acid mine drainage is a major problem in the West. Over half of impaired streams are contaminated by metals, many from draining mines like the Claytons'.

"Since the lawsuit, the Clayton Sapphire Mine has managed to implement two treatments that have brought the drainage into compliance with federal standards by making limestone sidings of the channel and spreading carbon over the forest area to reduce contaminants. Therefore, there will be no more taxes levied against the Clayton Sapphire Mine for the foreseeable future.'"

While the rest of the family responded with a collective cheer, Eli quietly hugged his mom. He knew how much sleep she'd lost over the long-standing court case.

"I'm only sorry that Dad isn't here to celebrate with us," Wymon continued. "With the money we're going to save, we'll be able to buy more cattle and build some much-needed holding pens."

Roce got up and gave Wymon a bear hug. "You're the best, bro."

Their mother rose to her feet, as well. "This is

the news our family has been waiting three years for. Wymon, I want to thank you from the bottom of my heart for doing a wonderful job of taking the reins at such a painful time and despite great personal sacrifice.

"And I want to thank all of my sons for working tirelessly alongside the stockmen and Luis to bring continued success to this ranch. I'm sure your father is rejoicing up in Heaven."

His heart brimming with emotion, Eli added his thoughts. "I, too, want to thank Wymon for his leadership and courage during a difficult period. I also want to thank all of you for helping me through a very dark time in my life. Libby couldn't have been born into a greater family. Mom has been a saint, and Solana has been right there with her this whole time, too."

Suddenly Toly spoke up. "Amen to everything Eli just said. And thanks to all of you for supporting my selfish ambition to make it to Las Vegas. If I get there, it will be my last attempt to win the gold buckle. After that, I'm coming home to ranch full-time again. I won't forget what you've all sacrificed for me."

"We're proud of you," Wymon added. "And now, Solana has prepared a feast. Let's head to the dining room, shall we?"

Luis joined them and they celebrated with a toast to the future. Once lunch was over, Eli was getting ready to leave for his house when his mother asked him to go upstairs with her.

Curious as to what she had to say, he followed her

up to her room. She closed the bedroom door before facing him with a sober look in her eyes.

"Mom?" he asked, his heart rate picking up. "What's wrong?"

"Sit down for a minute."

He frowned but snagged a chair while she sat on the side of her bed. "Is this about Tessa and Libby?"

She sat straight with her hands on her knees. "Yes. We haven't talked since you left for California yesterday. No one knows you went. Did you give Brianna the ring?"

"Yes. If you could have seen her eyes…"

"I can imagine. Have you set a date yet?"

"We didn't have time, but she'll be flying in tomorrow evening and we'll discuss it then."

A deep sigh escaped her lips. "That's what I need to talk to you about."

"Why do I get the feeling I'm not going to like this?"

She got up from the bed. "I wish your father were here. This is the hardest thing I've ever had to do."

Eli didn't like hearing that. "You've never minced words, Mom. Don't do it now."

"After Tessa put Libby down yesterday, she asked me to come over to the house for a talk. I thought it had something to do with your daughter, but nothing could be further from the truth."

He waited.

"Tessa told me she wishes she was still married to you. She says she knows she made a mistake in divorcing you and insists her feelings for you have come back even stronger than before."

Eli shook his head. "No. That's her fear talking because she's still afraid to be alone with Libby. This insecurity will pass with time."

"Wait before you say anything else, honey. She asked me to intervene for her."

Anger built inside of him. "In what way?"

"She begged me to talk to you about breaking it off with Brianna."

He bristled.

"You told her yourself you've only known Brianna a month. Tessa doesn't believe your feelings for Brianna could be anything like your feelings for her when the two of you got married. She wants the chance for the three of you to be a real family again. Being with you these last three weeks has been a revelation to her and—"

"Mom?" he broke in on her. "Do you hear yourself?"

"I'm only repeating what she said to me. She wishes she hadn't gotten sick, but she swears she's all better now and she wants her life back. She wants her daughter *and* her husband."

Eli flew out of the chair. "I'm not that man anymore."

"Just finish hearing me out, son."

"There's nothing more to hear."

"Except this… Remember when she told you she didn't want to be married anymore and how much that hurt you? Well, think about it—a year later she's come out of her deep depression and now that she's in her right state of mind, she knows what it is she truly wants. And now it's *you* who's saying you don't want it. All I'm asking is that you think about this long and hard. I just want you to be sure you won't change your mind down the road and wish you'd kept your family together."

"I'm desperately in love with Brianna."

His mother cocked her head. "Isn't it interesting that Brianna was the one who urged you to try again with Tessa?"

"Which I did. Nothing's there, believe me."

"I hear you. All I'm doing is conveying the message that Tessa wanted me to give you."

"It's too late."

"Eli—"

"She shouldn't have asked you to interfere. It's not fair for her to fall back on your love for her to try to fix a problem that can't be fixed. I've been doing my best to help her bond with Libby, but that's as far as things go between us." He gave his mother a kiss and left the bedroom.

Instead of rejoining his brothers, he found his parka and left through the back door. The short walk to his house helped him get his emotions under some semblance of control.

Tessa was cleaning up the kitchen when he walked in. She darted a glance at him. "Libby had her lunch and I put her down for a nap."

"Good. That gives us the time to talk."

She acted nervous. "I...take it your mother said something to you."

"Yup." Eli removed his parka. "Let's go in the living room."

He perched on the arm of the couch while she started picking up toys off the floor and putting them into a basket. She finally met his gaze. "I can tell you're upset and I don't blame you, but I was afraid to approach you."

"None of that matters, Tessa. Our marriage is over and has been for a long time. Last night I flew to California and gave Brianna an engagement ring."

"*That's* where you went?"

He nodded, registering her shock. "We're planning to be married soon. She left three weeks ago in order to give you and Libby a better chance to bond, but she's coming back tomorrow. Once she and I have returned from our honeymoon, we'll work out visitation."

"But you and I were a family once." He heard tears in her voice.

Eli got to his feet. "A year ago we were in a totally different place. I can't tell you how thankful I am that you want to be a mother to Libby. But you and I have changed. One day you'll meet a great guy who will make you happy and whole again. Someone who will learn to love Libby as much as you do."

She got up from the floor. "So Brianna's the love of your life."

He eyed her frankly. "Yes."

"And you're ready to get married so soon after meeting her? Aren't you afraid it might not last?"

"No. What we feel for each other is deep and real. My only concern is that you and Libby continue to get comfortable so that she'll be fine staying overnight with you, without me being there. That's the goal, right?"

Tessa's cheeks grew flushed.

"As long as Libby is still asleep, I have an errand to run. I'll be back at dinner." Without waiting for a response from Tessa, he walked into the kitchen to retrieve his parka before leaving the house.

Once in the truck, he drove into town and pulled up in front of the saddlery to talk to Clark Frost. This was a visit he couldn't put off.

Brianna's uncle had two customers. Eli checked out some of the saddles on display. The minute the last person left the store, he walked over to the older man, who smiled at him.

"Eli! Haven't seen you in a while." They shook hands. "What brings you in here?"

That question told him Brianna hadn't told her uncle about their engagement yet. She probably planned to phone later that day after her aunt and uncle came home from work.

"I got here as soon as I could to tell you something important. Last evening, I flew to California and celebrated part of Brianna's birthday with her."

"You what?"

"It was a very short trip because I had to be back for a business meeting at the ranch this morning. To get straight to the point, Brianna and I are now officially engaged. I know how much she loves you so I came right away to tell you. Besides my mother and ex-wife, you and her brother and his wife are the only other people to know yet."

"You got engaged…" Clark repeated it as if he was talking to himself. His reaction wasn't reassuring.

While the older man stood there, visibly stunned by the news, a couple came into the store. Eli would have to make this quick.

"I adore your niece and I gave her a ring with a blue sapphire from the mine. We're hoping to plan our wedding soon. But you're busy now and I have to get back to Libby. We'll talk again later after Brianna calls you with the news. Give my best to your wife."

Eli walked out of there, realizing he'd dropped a bombshell.

Her family knew why Brianna had gone to Marysville. No doubt they had ideas that, after Eli spent time alone with his ex-wife and daughter, the three of them might end up a family again, leaving Brianna on her own.

The more he thought about it, the more he realized that the people closest to him were probably thinking, maybe even hoping, that that would happen. He couldn't blame them. A year ago, he would have given anything for Tessa to recover and come back home.

But not anymore. His heart was with someone else.

He got in his truck and headed to a drive-through to get a coffee. After finding a parking space around back, he phoned Brianna, needing to hear her voice.

She picked up on the third ring. "Eli?"

"Sweetheart?"

"I'm so glad you called," she said softly. "I'll be coming in on the five-thirty evening flight."

"I'll be there to pick you up. But first you need to know I just dropped by the saddlery to tell your uncle we're engaged. I'd assumed he already knew, but I was mistaken."

He heard a slight gasp. "I was waiting to tell them tonight when I phoned to let them know I'll be home tomorrow." Brianna knew her uncle wouldn't be thrilled about the news.

"I'm glad he knows," Eli said.

"You're right that he had to be told. Oh, Eli, do you really think it will be okay for me to come home now?"

"I *know* it will be," he assured her. They'd followed the doctor's advice for these past three weeks. But the game plan had changed because Eli hadn't expected that Tessa would start to get ideas about rekindling their marriage.

"Is Libby acting like a daughter around Tessa?"

"To some degree."

"That's good news."

"The good news is that you're coming home. I can't live without you any longer."

"Same here. As soon as we get off the phone I'll call my aunt and uncle and let them know I'm coming."

"I love you," Eli said in a husky voice. "We need to start working on those wedding plans."

"I'm way ahead of you."

His heart leaped. "Phone me later. I'm heading back to the ranch now. I'll be listening for your call."

"You're my whole world, Eli."

"Oh, Brianna." He sighed. "You don't know how good it feels to hear you say that."

Chapter Ten

Later that afternoon, Brianna grabbed her suitcase off the carousel and hurried out the main doors of the Missoula airport into the freezing cold air.

She spotted Eli's truck right away and headed in its direction. The tall, gorgeous rancher saw her coming and stepped out onto the sidewalk. Her heart thudded out of control.

"You're home!" he cried, picking her up and swinging her around. In front of all the other cars, he kissed her long and hard.

"I've been living for this," she whispered against his cheek.

"Come on." He reached for her suitcase and walked her to the truck with his arm around her shoulders. "Someone's waiting to see you."

"You brought Libby?"

He opened the rear door and there sat his adorable daughter all bundled up in her car seat. The second she saw who it was she cried out, *"Bree! Bree!"*

The joy in her voice warmed Brianna's heart. She hadn't forgotten her. "Darling girl. It's so wonderful to see you!" She leaned in and kissed her on both cheeks.

Libby wanted to get out and held up her arms for someone to pick her up, but Eli intervened. "You have to stay where you are until we take Brianna home." He kissed her brown curls. After putting the suitcase on the other side of the seat, he closed the door and helped Brianna into the truck, kissing her again before starting the engine.

He clasped her hand all the way to the Frosts' house. Meanwhile, Libby had a meltdown in the backseat.

"I'm right here, Libby. Oh, Eli. She's so upset."

"She'll get over it in a hurry as soon as we reach your aunt and uncle's house. I want them to realize the three of us are going to be a family. Libby adores you, and I want them to see that."

Between Libby's crying and Taffy's barking, the reunion with the Frosts was noisy and chaotic until Brianna finally picked Libby up. Then her tears magically disappeared.

Everyone gathered in the living room in front of the fire. Brianna removed Libby's parka and sat down in the easy chair with her. The dog crept closer to sniff and lick both of them, causing Libby to giggle. Then the little girl caught sight of the sapphire ring and grabbed Brianna's hand.

"This is something new, huh, Libby? Your daddy gave it to me. That big blue heart came from your family's sapphire mine." Libby looked up at her. "It's my ring. Can you say *ring*?"

"Reen."

Brianna's gaze collided with Eli's. He said, "That's the seventh word to come out of her mouth. She can say *ring* now. And notice how she's pronouncing the *n*?"

"That's right! Good job, sweetie." She kissed her again. "Ring. Do you want to hold it?" Brianna slipped it off her finger and let Eli's daughter examine it. Libby kept trying to put it on her own fingers with no luck. Everyone laughed. "It's too big. We'll have to get you your own ring one of these days."

Her aunt Joanne walked over and hugged the two of them. "Congratulations on your engagement. You too, Eli." He was sitting on the chair next to them and she hugged him, as well. "We couldn't be happier with the news, right, Clark?"

"Absolutely. By marrying Eli, we're going to have our niece living close by for the rest of our lives. There could be no greater blessing. Welcome to the family, Eli." Brianna was overjoyed that her uncle was taking the announcement so well.

"Thank you. Libby and I have been waiting for this day from the first time the three of us met. It was love at first sight. I intend to love your niece for the rest of her days and make her as happy as she makes me."

"Have you two set a date?" her uncle asked.

"Not yet, Uncle Clark." She put the ring back on her finger. "We'll have to look at a time that's good for everyone on both sides of our families."

"We want it to be soon," Eli added.

Brianna let Libby get down off her lap so she could

pet the dog. "I told Doug we'd probably get married at the church here in town and have a reception. He and Carol offered to hold an open house later in the year for our friends in Marysville, but nothing's been decided for sure." She looked at her uncle. "Will you give me away, Uncle Clark?"

His eyes misted over. "It will be a great honor."

"Can I offer your daughter a cookie, Eli?" Aunt Joanne asked.

His smile turned Brianna's heart over. "She'd love it."

"Okay, let me just run to the kitchen. Be right back."

Her aunt returned quickly and knelt next to Libby, who was patting Taffy. Clearly the dog loved the attention. "Would you like a treat?" The sound of that word caused the dog to lift her head.

Libby studied the sugar cookie before taking it from her. After biting into it, she broke off a piece to feed the dog. Then she took another bite and the whole process began again.

Eli chuckled. "I'm afraid she thinks eating is a game. I take a bite and she takes a bite. We do it all the time."

"She's precious," Brianna's aunt murmured.

"Guess what, Aunt Joanne? Libby has spotted your pink sapphire ring and can't take her eyes off it."

Her aunt put her right hand in front of Libby, who touched the stone. "Do you like my ring?"

"Reen," Libby said again.

"It came from your family's sapphire mine, too."
She smiled at Brianna. "We're two lucky women."

"You can say that again." Brianna was so happy
that she felt as if she could burst.

By now Libby was toddling around the living room
inspecting everything. The dog followed close behind, causing them to chuckle. Eli's little girl had
won her family over to the fact that a wedding was
going to take place. Eli's decision to bring her to the
house had been the perfect way to break the ice with
her uncle.

When Libby started removing magazines from
the basket in which they were housed, Eli scooped
her up in his arms. "I think my little cowgirl has had
enough excitement for one day and needs to go home
for dinner and bed."

Brianna's heart fell. She didn't want the evening
to end, but she knew this was one time she had no
choice. She was acutely aware of the fact that Tessa
would be waiting at home for them. Reaching for
Libby's miniature parka, she helped Eli put it on his
daughter.

Eli said good-night to her aunt and uncle and
then Brianna walked him to the foyer with Taffy at
her side. He kissed her, but it didn't last nearly long
enough. "I'll phone you in the morning and we'll
make plans for tomorrow."

"It's getting harder and harder to say good-night."
She half moaned the words.

"I know. It's close to impossible," he ground out.

"We need to pick a date tomorrow. I'm crazy in love with you."

"That's how I feel, exactly." She kissed him again and then Libby, but she didn't say good-bye in the hope that his daughter wouldn't cry because they had to leave.

No such luck. The second he opened the door and walked outside into the cold, Libby protested and cried all the way to his truck.

Brianna's heart couldn't take much more. Their wedding day couldn't come soon enough.

ELI SANG ONE song after another to entertain his daughter on the drive home. When they arrived at the ranch, he carried her into the house and discovered that Tessa was still awake. She got up from the couch, where she'd been watching TV.

"Hi. You're back kind of late."

"Yeah, sorry. She's ready for dinner. Then it's bedtime right away."

Tessa reached for her, but Libby hid her face in Eli's neck. It was the first time Libby hadn't gone to her since Tessa had started staying the night. He carried his daughter into the kitchen and put her in her high chair. Tessa got out the jars of baby food and fed her without a problem.

When Libby had finished eating, they walked through the house to the nursery.

Together they got her changed and tucked her into the crib with the new stuffed bunny Tessa had given her. To his relief Libby hugged it. The action had to please her mother.

Eli left the room first and went to the kitchen to make some coffee. "Would you like some?" he asked as Tessa walked in.

"No, thank you, but I'd like to talk to you."

"Go ahead."

"I smelled perfume on Libby's outfit. Just how close is our daughter to Brianna?"

The question had been inevitable. He chose his words carefully. "In her own way Libby loves her, and vice versa."

"That explains why she wouldn't hug me when you arrived back here."

"Tessa—she'll never be Libby's mother and could never take your place. But I'm glad they're getting close. That way Libby will always be happy whether she's with me or with you."

"How soon are you getting married?"

"We're going to discuss that tomorrow evening."

"So you won't be home again until late?"

"Probably not."

She leaned against the counter. "You must have some idea of a date."

"Hopefully mid-March. Maybe sooner depending on everyone's schedules."

"Is she going to continue working at the saddlery?"

He looked at her over the rim of the mug. "I don't know, but whatever we end up doing, nothing's going to interfere with the visitation schedule we set up."

"I've been thinking about that. It's not going to

work if we have to drive back and forth from Thompson Falls all the time. It's too long a trip. After talking it over with Mom and Dad, I've decided to move to Stevensville and get a condo."

Eli hadn't seen that coming.

"They'll finance it until I get a job and they're buying me a car, too. That way I can have Libby several times a week and every other weekend or one overnight every weekend. My doctor thinks it's a good idea, but only if I'm ready. I *know* I am."

Something fundamental had happened for Tessa to consider stepping out of her comfort zone, away from her family, and he had to admit the idea made a lot of sense.

"That's a big change for you. I agree it'll be a lot easier on both of us."

"So, you wouldn't mind if I moved here?"

"No, Tessa. I just want all of us to be happy."

"You don't think my living in town will bother Brianna?"

"No, I don't. I think she'll be relieved we don't have to make the long trip to Thompson Falls so often. But even if you don't find a condo you like right away, be assured that we'll do whatever it takes to make this work." He got up from the table and rinsed out his mug. "I have to be up at the crack of dawn, so I'm going to bed. Good night."

"Good night," she whispered.

EIGHTEEN HOURS LATER, Eli sat in the Frosts' living room while he and Brianna discussed wedding plans with her family after dinner. Because of a conflict with Toly's rodeo schedule, they chose March 18 as the date so everyone they loved could make it. The minister said the church in town would be available that Saturday and they were able to book the Stevensville Hotel for the reception.

Eli's first marriage and reception had taken place in Thompson Falls. Another reception had followed the next evening at the Clayton ranch house. His marriage to Brianna would be different and exactly the way she wanted it.

Still needing to settle some details, they left her family to talk things over with Eli's mother. But when Eli got Brianna into his truck, he didn't start it up right away. Instead, he pulled her over so she was half sitting on his lap. They kissed with a hunger that was growing out of control. He finally lifted his head. "Now that our plans are made, there's something important I have to tell you."

"If you're worried that we're not going to have a long honeymoon because of Libby, don't be. I don't care about that as long as I'm your wife. There'll be time for a trip later on in the year when she feels totally secure being away from you."

"You're one amazing woman, Brianna Frost. But this is about something else. Last night Tessa wanted to talk after we put Libby to bed."

Her blue eyes searched his. "You sound concerned."

"She's planning to move here and get a condo in town."

Hearing those words, Brianna sat up and turned to him. "I can understand why she wants to do it. Don't you?"

"Yes, and it makes sense. During our marriage she made friends here, so it won't be as if she feels completely isolated. What's bothering me is that she's now in competition with you for Libby's affection. Last night our daughter didn't go to Tessa when we walked in the house." He hadn't told Brianna that Tessa wanted to get remarried to him. No way did he intend to tell her that.

Brianna groaned. "I suppose that was inevitable."

"I'm convinced that no matter how long you stayed away, Tessa would still feel threatened. It's something we have to deal with and not let it impact our plans."

"I agree. But I feel sorry for Tessa. She's lost a whole year."

"I know. Let's just be thankful she has her doctor, who's going to continue to work with her. In the meantime, all we can do is go on with our plans and do what has to be done. I only told you this so you'll be aware of her feelings."

"I think her feelings are normal and I'd probably be just as threatened if our positions were reversed. I'll be as careful and sensitive as I can."

"You think I don't know that?" He clasped her to him, burying his face in her hair. "Let's change the subject. I thought this coming weekend we'd start tearing the house apart and paint it throughout with a color scheme we both want. Nothing's been done to the house, except for the nursery, since my grandparents lived there for the last twenty-five years of their lives."

"You're kidding."

"Nope. I'm letting Sarah go after the wedding and sending her a check for three months' wages. I hope that will leave her with enough money so she won't worry until she finds a new job.

"The rest of the money I set aside for a nanny can now go to transforming this house into *our* house. Tessa and I got married fast with zero money to our names and were grateful the family let us move in here just as it was. But that's in the past.

"I want us to buy new furniture, art we both love, new windows and window coverings and carpeting— the works! I'd like you to design the master bedroom. I'm sure there are things your parents left you. Use them any way you want throughout the house. All the old things we'll put in storage at the ranch house for any family member who might need them in the future."

For her response, she hugged him so hard around the neck that she practically cut off his breathing. "When I went to bed last night, my aunt hinted that they were going to buy us a car for a wedding present. She told me to think about the kind we wanted that would be best for Libby."

Eli sent up a silent thanks for Clark's wife, who was in their corner. Eli had a hunch it was going to take longer to win Clark over completely. Clark and Eli's father had shared confidences over the years. Unfortunately Clark hadn't been fed the right information about the circumstances surrounding Eli's first marriage. One of these days he'd pull him aside and tell him the truth.

"Come on. I'd better get you home. Do you know how great it's going to be when we get to go home together? Give me one more kiss so I can make it through tonight." Since Brianna had come into his life, he couldn't imagine having to live much longer without her.

On Saturday Eli had asked Wymon to help him move the furniture out of the master bedroom. Brianna did her part, dressed in an old T-shirt and a torn pair of jeans. They loaded two trucks to the brim and drove them to the ranch house. Until their new California king–size bed arrived the next Saturday, Eli would be sleeping in the guest room.

"We'll be gone until after lunch," Eli said to Brianna.

"Take your time. I've got a ton of work to do here."

He swept her into his arms, kissing her breathless before leaving the house. After he left, she freshened up in the bathroom and removed her ring. Now she was ready to start painting and walked into the master bedroom to get started. She tuned the radio to a soft rock station and spread some drop sheets on the floor. Some cans of primer sat in one corner.

After sorting through dozens of paint samples, they'd settled on lemon white for the master bedroom walls.

Gone were the old curtains. The new bedroom

furniture would be coming in a mellow cream color. She and her aunt had picked out the most gorgeous quilt in a Western motif. Talk about the room being transformed!

She poured paint in the tray and dipped the roller in it, and then she began applying the first coat to the walls. Eli had already filled all the nail holes and sanded them.

When the first wall was finished, she took a break and went down the hall to the bathroom. When she came out again, she saw Tessa standing at the end of the hall with a pile of folded clothes in her arms. Brianna stopped in her tracks.

"Oh—you surprised me!"

"Hi, Tessa. I didn't realize you were here." Eli had told her his ex-wife was staying at the ranch house with Libby and his mom for the weekend, but there was no sign of their little girl with her.

"I just thought I'd come over and finish the wash while Eli's mom is watching Libby. Maybe Eli told you Sarah isn't working for him anymore, so I've taken over the household duties. I was just about to put Libby's clean clothes in her drawers."

Brianna blinked. She was pretty certain Eli hadn't expected her to come over here today while they were working on the house, but Brianna didn't want to make her feel unwelcome.

"No problem," she told her. "Go ahead and do what you need to do."

Trying not to let Tessa's presence bother her, Brianna went to the bedroom and started painting the next wall. She'd barely gotten started when Tessa appeared in the doorway.

"You've gotten busy in a hurry."

Brianna was surprised at the comment but chose not to let it get to her. "The wedding isn't that far off. We're planning to paint all the rooms."

"I wanted to transform the house. This room was always so dark. But after I got pregnant, I had terrible morning sickness and couldn't be around paint so we had to let that project go."

Brianna thought she knew where Tessa was going with this but blathered on nervously. "My friend had morning sickness for a while. I know it can be bad."

"You have no idea." Tessa paused a moment and then asked, "As long as I'm here, do you mind if I talk to you?"

"Sure," she said and turned off the radio she'd placed on the stepladder. As she did so, Tessa said, "I understand he's given you a sapphire from the mine."

"Yes. He surprised me with it when he flew to California for my birthday."

"A heart for an engagement ring. How unusual."

"I was born on Valentine's Day."

"You're kidding."

Brianna took a quick breath. "Tessa, I'm sure you're anxious to talk to me about the visitation schedule for Libby. I'm willing to work out anything you want, as far as that goes."

"I appreciate that, but there's something else I have to say. Brianna... I still love Eli."

She knew it.

"My illness caused a chemical reaction in me, but when he brought Libby to see me, it was like I'd awakened from a deep sleep."

With those words, Brianna put the roller down, her hand shaking too much to paint. "Why don't we go in the living room," she said and walked into the hall. Tessa followed her.

"Eli didn't want the divorce."

"I know. He's told me everything."

"No doubt. I don't blame him for dating you. I told him our marriage was over, and he finally took me at my word. But I've recovered from my illness now. I never dreamed I'd be stricken by the kind of depression I had, but it's over and I want my family back."

Brianna sank down in one of the living room chairs.

Tessa stood in front of her, her whole body pleading. "As one woman to another, I'm begging you to call off your engagement so Eli and I can have a real chance to put our marriage back together. He says he loves you and I believe him, but I know deep down he still cares for me. Otherwise he wouldn't have let me live here with him while you were away.

"Let me ask you a question. If you were in my shoes, would you give up on your marriage so easily after knowing that your illness made you say and do things that you wouldn't normally do? Wouldn't you fight for Eli with every breath in your body before it was too late?"

Yes, she would.

"That's what I'm doing now. Did Eli tell you I

spoke to him about getting remarried? We talked the other night and I begged him to reconsider what he's doing. If he didn't tell you about our talk yet, that means he's thinking hard about it."

Brianna didn't know. He hadn't said anything to her.

"Both our families want to see us back together. That hasn't changed. It's the reason I've come to you. Please consider carefully everything I've said. You don't have a daughter. Your life isn't on the line in the same way.

"It was as if a miracle happened when he came to my door that day. At first I sent him away, but that was because I was in shock. As the day wore on, I felt like I'd been let out of prison and was free to be myself for the first time in a year."

Brianna feared that if she was forced to listen to any more it would kill her. She got up from her chair and stared out the window. Her words from a few weeks ago came back to torture her. *Don't give up on winning your wife back. The chemistry in the brain can change. Good-bye, Eli Clayton. You're the best.*

Taking a fortifying breath, she turned to Tessa. "I wouldn't wish the experience you've been through this last year on anyone. I promise I'll think about everything you said."

"Thank you for listening to me. I'd better go."

She put on her parka and left the house. Brianna watched through the window until Tessa was out of sight. Then she went back to the bedroom to finish painting the rest of the wall. When it was done, she put the lid on the can and washed out the roller and tray in the kitchen sink.

Eli still hadn't returned. It gave her time to freshen up and put her ring back on. After slipping on her coat, she left the house and got in the truck to head back to Stevensville.

When she looked down, the light from outside had captured the facets of the sapphire on her ring.

That's my heart, he'd said.

But did he truly mean it?

Chapter Eleven

There was one person Brianna had to talk to and she needed to be alone to do it, where Eli couldn't walk in on her. When she reached her uncle's house, she hurried to her bedroom. To her relief her family had gone to visit friends and had taken Taffy with them.

Beyond tears, she phoned her brother.

Pick up, pick up.

"Brianna?"

"I'm so glad you answered."

"What's wrong?"

"Oh, Doug—everything is so horribly wrong, I don't know if I can marry Eli."

Silence prevailed before he said, "Are you thinking of calling off the wedding?"

Her pain had reached its zenith. "Is that what you think I should do, too?"

"Too? What are you talking about?"

"Eli's ex-wife wants her husband back. She came to the house earlier to ask me to walk away and give them a chance. She said both families are hoping for the same thing. If you'd heard the pain in her voice, you'd understand why I'm in such agony."

"Was she cruel to you?"

"Not cruel. Deep down I know she's hurt that Eli has found someone else. I know she's anxious. All she did was plead for her life back with Eli. Let's be honest. She couldn't help the depression that changed her. But it's gone now and she wants them to be a family again. At least she was honest with me. How can I stand in the way of that?"

"I'm sorry her illness changed their lives. But now Eli loves *you,* Brianna. Carol and I can see it and feel it."

"But he loved her first and married her. Now that she's not ill anymore, she wants to honor the vows she made to him and keep their family intact. Libby needs her parents."

"She has them and always will, no matter the situation. Does Eli know about today's conversation?"

"Not unless she's already told him."

"Where are you?"

"I left Eli's house and came home. Uncle Clark and Aunt Joanne aren't here right now."

"Do yourself a favor and don't tell anyone about this until you talk to Eli. He deserves to know everything. I like the guy a lot. So does Carol."

"I'm so glad, but apparently Tessa did talk to him about how she feels and he chose not to tell me. What does that say about him?"

"Tessa has put him in a difficult position, but you're the woman he's planning to marry. Get on the phone to him as soon as we hang up and straighten this out before it causes real trouble," her brother said.

She gripped the phone tighter. "I'm scared, Doug."

"About what? Surely you don't doubt that he loves you."

"No. It's actually something I said to Eli weeks ago after telling him I wouldn't go out with him anymore."

"What was that?"

"I—I told him to fight for his marriage," she stammered. "I told him a miracle could happen. And now it *has*. She wants him back. If I don't step away, then—"

"Then you've deduced that you're a terrible person for interfering with the miracle. I know how your mind works. Don't take on guilt and do this to yourself. Eli loves you. Brianna? Are you listening to me? If you run away now, then you're not the strong woman he adores or the strong sister I know you to be."

"But if you could have heard her."

"I swear if you don't call Eli right now, I'll call him myself and then get on the next plane for Missoula if necessary. Do you hear what I'm saying?"

It took her the longest time before she could respond. "I'll do it."

"Don't make a promise you can't keep."

He always said that.

"I promise. I love you, Doug." Tears pooled in her eyes and started running down her cheeks.

Before she lost her nerve, she hung up and phoned

Eli. He answered on the third ring. "Hi, my love. I know I'm late, but we had to rearrange the storage room before we could fit all the new stuff inside. It took forever, but now it's done. I'll be at the house in a few minutes."

She held her breath. "Eli? I'm not there. I left and drove to my uncle's for a clean change of clothes. I had an accident and got paint on my blouse and jeans. But I'm leaving now and will meet you there ASAP."

"Okay, hurry!" he said.

She clicked off and sat with her head in her hands for a minute. Then she went to her closet and swapped out her clothes before walking back to the truck, resigned to meeting her fate.

AFTER DROPPING WYMON at his place, Eli drove to his own house. When he walked inside, he discovered Brianna had painted two of the four bedroom walls with the primer before she'd had her accident.

He turned on the radio and decided to put on the first coat of paint over the dried primer while he waited for her. His heart raced when she walked in a few minutes later wearing a white T-shirt and jeans, her outfit hugging her curves in all the right places.

She came right over and kissed him on the neck. "I'm so glad you're back. I missed you this morning."

"I didn't mean to be so long. You've done a great job on these walls."

"Thanks. I would have painted all of them, but I had a visitor." She poured more primer into the pan and reached for the other roller.

"Who was that?"

"Tessa."

Eli kept the roller moving evenly. "Did she come to get some of Libby's toys?"

"No. She was finishing up the laundry and put some clothes away in Libby's room."

He frowned and looked over at her. "She shouldn't have been here at all. Was Libby with her?"

"No. She said your mom was watching her. I could tell that doing the laundry was an excuse for her to talk to me."

When she knew he wouldn't be there.

Bristling with an anger he'd never felt before, Eli finished the wall he'd been working on and put the roller down. "Brianna?"

"Yes?" She'd started painting as if nothing was wrong, but he knew differently.

"Hell," he swore softly. "My hope that Tessa wouldn't be brazen enough to approach you on your own went up in smoke today, didn't it?"

"I'll admit I was surprised she'd come in the house. Why didn't you tell me she's already told you that she wants you back?"

He expelled his breath. "Because I don't care what she wants and told her as much. I'm sorry, Brianna. She knew Wymon and I were busy, and she no doubt saw this as her last chance to get me back. She probably told Mom she wanted to talk to you about visitation and my mother agreed to stay with Libby until she got back."

"I can tell your mom loves her very much."

"She does and always will, but I'm sure Mom had no idea of her true intentions today. Tessa's tendency to push the envelope hasn't changed, despite her illness. If anything, she's shown an incredible amount of willfulness. You and I have been over this before, but I'm going to tell you a few things I didn't tell you the first time."

"About what? She only wants what any woman would want after what she's been through."

"Both parties have to want the same thing, Brianna. When Tessa and I were dating, she demanded that I marry her right away or I would lose her. I saw a selfishness in her that surprised me. She wasn't willing to wait a year, even though we needed the money my time on the circuit would provide. Her ultimatum disturbed me and I needed time to think about it.

"Here's the part you *don't* know. When I came back to find her ill with the flu, she implied that if I hadn't left, she probably wouldn't have gotten so sick. Looking back now, I realize she wanted me to feel guilty so I would cave and agree to get married. Do you hear what I'm saying?"

She was slow to nod, hopefully a sign that he was getting through to her.

"Tessa asked me to break off my engagement to you," she said.

"What did you say to her?"

"I told her I'd talk to you."

He shook his head. "When she came out of that depression, what she hadn't counted on was the fact that my feelings for her had died during the hellish year we'd lived through. I'm sorry it happened, but her illness changed everything.

"And there's still one trait about Tessa that hasn't changed—she wants what she wants when she wants it. I see a little bit of that in Libby. We'll have to work on it with her. This time, however, Tessa can't have everything she wants and she will have to make a new life with someone else if she wants to get married again."

"She's a good person."

"I agree, and she'll always have a piece of my heart. But that was another world and another time. *You're* the woman I'm in love with. Together we'll keep each other happy and have more babies. Libby's going to need a brother or sister. We'll shower her with love. Tessa will give her the love she needs from her mom. It will work out, all of it."

Brianna finished painting the wall and put the roller down, looking haunted.

"What is it?"

"You make it sound so easy, but she said both families wanted the two of you to get back together."

"Of course they did in the beginning. Her condition was a tragedy that shouldn't have happened, but it did. Now I'm going to tell you something my mother told me when I bought the heart sapphire right after you left for California. She said she'd decided never to sell it but changed her mind when she saw the way we looked at each other. She said it was as if two pairs of blue eyes glowed like flames. She knew at that moment that what we had was magical."

Brianna's face lit up. "She really told you that?"

"Cross my heart, you beautiful creature. Do you honestly believe she would have said those words, or let me give you that ring, if she didn't want you to be her new daughter-in-law? I'll tell you something else. She gave us that stone as her wedding present to us."

Taking advantage of Brianna being at a loss for words, he reached for her. "So now you've got two choices. You can get on a plane with me tonight. We'll fly to Las Vegas and get married. That's my personal choice."

He heard a moan before Brianna started to cover his face with kisses. "What's my other choice?"

"To go ahead with our plans for a March wedding and make everyone happy. At least they will be, after I have a little chat with your uncle."

Her heart was in her eyes. "I'm glad you're going to tell him the whole truth. Uncle Clark takes his job as my protector seriously."

"Don't I know it. Your aunt had to provoke him into congratulating us."

"No, she didn't," Brianna said, but her words came out muffled against his neck.

He laughed. "He's about as subtle as a mounted bull rider ready to slaughter the competition. I have a feeling he left dead bodies all over the arena when he used to compete. Was your father the same way?"

She cupped his jaw with her hand. "The two of them were pretty equal in the tough dude department, but Dad had a bit of a softer side. Doug and I ruined him."

"Well, we've got Libby, who's going to turn your family's house upside down. No doubt Grandpa Frost will morph into such a marshmallow that we won't recognize him."

A giggle burst out of her, the happy kind he'd wondered if he'd ever hear again when they'd first started talking.

"Come on. The rest of the painting can wait for another day. You drive back to your uncle's. I'll be there after I've cleaned up the paint and showered. Once I've talked to Clark and put his mind at rest, there'll be nothing stopping us. What do you say?"

She pressed her mouth to his. "I'm praying for March to get here *fast*."

"You don't know the half of it."

Twenty minutes later, he pulled up to the ranch house and went in search of Tessa. He found her upstairs in the guest bedroom. She saw him out in the hall and got off the phone. Eli was glad his daughter wasn't with her.

"I'm glad you're free for a minute. We need to talk."

"Uh-oh. I can tell you're upset with me for talking to Brianna."

"Not upset. Let's go to the study where we can have privacy."

They made it downstairs without Libby spotting them. He imagined she was in the kitchen with his mother and Solana.

"After you," he said waving Tessa inside his father's den and shutting the door behind them. "Go ahead and sit down."

He perched on the end of the couch while she sat in one of the overstuffed leather chairs. "You told her you still love me. I don't doubt that you care, but it's not love. In fact, I'm not sure it ever was, not in the deepest sense of the word. You wanted to get married. Your friends were getting married. It seemed the exciting thing to do. Am I right?"

She stared at him for a long time before nodding.

"I didn't want to lose you, so we got married. But our year apart changed everything, except our love for Libby."

"I know, but I've been confused since you brought her to see me. Forgive me for what I said today."

"You were being honest, so there's nothing to forgive, Tessa. More importantly, there's something vital you should know. Brianna urged me to try and reconnect with you so you and Libby could have a relationship. *She's* the reason I went to see you in Thompson Falls in the first place."

At that revelation Tessa's complexion paled.

"Her parents were killed in a car crash almost a year ago. She has cried to me over her loss so many times. Brianna and her mother were very close and she'll miss her every day for the rest of her life. When she begged me to go see you and take Libby, it was because she knew what it would mean to our daughter one day to have a loving mother, the kind Brianna had. The kind *you* have. The kind *I* have.

"The woman I'm engaged to has always put you

and Libby first. You'll never have to worry about her trying to undermine you. I'd like to think that the woman I was once married to will respect Brianna for the big part she'll play in Libby's life. Our daughter is going to need all of us to pull together."

Tears glimmered in Tessa's eyes. "You really are in love. I can feel it. I'm so sorry for approaching her today. I'll apologize to her. Brianna Frost is a very lucky woman."

"She says the same thing about you because Libby is your little girl and Brianna adores her. Libby's the best part of both of us, Tessa."

She rose to her feet. "I know." Her voice trembled. "I'm going to go find Libby right now. God bless you and Brianna, Eli."

He followed her out of the study but left the house through the front door and raced to his truck. In his heart Eli knew there'd be no more trouble with Tessa. His biggest concern was to get Clark Frost on his side.

Chapter Twelve

It was almost Eli's wedding day! He came down from the range Friday after work, jubilant that this would be his last night alone. Tomorrow Brianna would become his wife.

His clunky truck creaked and groaned as he made the turns. It was on its last legs but had served him well. He'd bought it used on his sixteenth birthday with his own money. One of these days he'd invest in a new one, but he and Brianna would work it into the budget later in the year. He was thankful her aunt and uncle had bought her a new car.

For the moment, he and Brianna were using his money to finish up the rest of the changes to the house. He loved Brianna's taste. Already, the house looked like a completely different place. Halfway home he received a text from Roce:

Hey, bro. TGIF party in the barn. You'd better show up pronto because you're already ten minutes late!

He let out a bark of laughter. His brothers were throwing him a bachelor party in the barn tonight?

Trust them to keep him in the dark. His excitement over the wedding caused him to drive too fast. When he pulled up to the barn, he had to apply the brakes before he drove right through the closed doors. Their squeal resounded in the cold night air.

No one seemed to be around. What was going on in there? He parked the car over by the corral fence and then jumped down from the cab and rushed to open the doors.

"*Surprise!*"

To his shock, he saw all three of his brothers standing in the bed of a brand-new Silverado 1500 full-size four-door black truck parked at an angle inside the entrance. If he didn't know better, he would think he was face-to-face with a giant dealership ad.

He took a step back. "That's a lot of manhood I'm looking at."

Toly grinned. "You're supposed to be looking at the truck!"

"It's yours, bro." This from Roce.

Eli's heart almost failed him.

His big brother, Wymon, flashed him a rare smile. "No one has worked harder than you this year to earn it. Climb in and show us what it can do. The key is in the ignition. Let's be sure it can take you and that gorgeous bride-to-be of yours on your honeymoon without a problem."

This gift was totally unexpected. Eli was so humbled by their generosity that he couldn't talk for a minute. "I can't accept it."

"The hell you can't!" they said in unison.

Luis suddenly appeared at the entrance. "You'd better do as they say. Your brothers mean business."

"So you were in on this, too."

"I just do what I'm told. For what it's worth, no one deserves this more than you. Luke says the same thing. That's the highest praise coming from him. Go on. I'll shut the doors after you leave."

With a whoop, Eli leaped into the cab. The smell of a brand-new truck was like nothing else on earth. So was the feel of so much power as he drove them up the mountain. When there was too much snow to go any farther, he parked the truck and got out.

As his brothers jumped down, he hugged each one. Together they looked out at the magnificent Sapphire Mountain range silhouetted against the night sky.

"I don't know how to thank you guys," he said in a husky voice. "I'll never forget it."

"Don't worry. We won't let you," Roce teased him.

They all laughed, but this time his brothers climbed into the cab for the drive back. Eli suddenly realized it was freezing out. But he was so on fire for Brianna that he'd been oblivious. Tomorrow was almost here. He could hardly breathe.

BRIANNA'S AUNT AND uncle had lived and worked in Stevensville for years. Between all their friends and those of the Claytons, the church didn't even have standing room by the time the three o'clock ceremony was set to begin. Brianna was stunned at the overflow. She couldn't see Eli for all the people.

The organist had begun playing as Brianna's uncle helped her inside the foyer with her bouquet of yellow and white roses. She wore a white silk wedding dress she and her aunt had bought after a quick trip to Missoula. It was a princess design with short sleeves and a scooped neck. A shoulder-length lace veil partially covered her hair.

"Don't be nervous," her uncle whispered. "I can see Eli and Wymon at the altar waiting for you."

She knew Eli had wanted his older brother to stand up for him. Brianna had asked Carol and Lindsay to be her bridesmaids. They were both pregnant and looked lovely in pale yellow chiffon, but Lindsay was the only one showing.

Doug and Eli's other brothers acted as ushers. Libby was too little to come to the ceremony, but Eli's mother would bring her to the hotel for the dinner afterward.

"It's time, honey. Pretend I'm your dad."

She squeezed his arm. "No. You've been my other dad since the day I came to stay with you. You and Joanne are the greatest blessings in my life."

"And you're the daughter we never had. Shall we go and get you married now? If we don't start down the aisle, Eli's going to come striding back here to find out the reason for the hold up."

Brianna smiled up at him. Eli and her uncle had become good friends since the night Eli confided in him about his first marriage. Their talk had helped her uncle understand the truth about why Eli hadn't felt ready to get married the first time.

Once her bridesmaids began to make their way down the aisle, Brianna entered the chapel with her uncle and started her journey toward the ruggedly handsome cowboy she'd loved from day one. He stood tall in a formal, navy blue suit and white shirt with a yellow rose in his lapel.

His dark blue eyes lit up as she drew closer to him. He grasped her hand and mouthed, *I love you*, before he walked her the rest of the way to where the minister waited for them. She stared at Eli and mouthed the same words back, feeling the warmth of his hand travel through her trembling body.

"Dearly beloved, what a glorious day for this man and woman to come together to become one in the sight of God and these witnesses."

Brianna heard the minister speaking, but so many thoughts were spinning in her head that she couldn't absorb them all until she heard him say, "I now pronounce you man and wife."

A gold wedding band had now joined her engagement ring. She'd given Eli a gold wedding band inlaid with small blue sapphires. Brianna had picked it out with his mother's help.

Before the minister could tell Eli to kiss his bride, Eli was already fulfilling that part of the ceremony. It was a husband's kiss he was giving her, so full of desire Brianna had to cling to him so she wouldn't fall.

The minister finally cleared his throat, and Eli took his time before releasing her mouth. "If you'll please turn to face your family and friends... May I present Mr. and Mrs. Eli Hartman Clayton! You may congratulate them in the foyer."

The length of their kiss had brought heat rushing to her cheeks and Brianna knew her face looked flushed as she smiled at her aunt and Eli's mother. It appeared that the whole congregation was smiling back. Eli gripped her waist. "I wish we could skip the reception," he whispered.

She noticed his brothers grinning as if they knew exactly what he'd just said.

"If we don't make an appearance, we'll miss seeing Libby," Brianna said.

"I spent all morning with her, but I wouldn't keep her from seeing you in that exquisite wedding dress. She'll think you're a princess come to life. My princess bride. I thank God for you, Brianna," he said, his voice shaking, before they worked their way down the aisle to the foyer.

Later at the hotel, Alberta walked Libby over to the head table. She wore a little yellow dress trimmed in eyelet and a yellow bow in her hair. Brianna saw her coming and turned to greet her.

Eli's little girl stared at her for the longest time. "Don't you know me? Maybe this will help." She carefully removed her veil and Eli took it from her. That did the trick.

"*Bree!*"

"Yes, darling. Come here." She pulled her on her lap. Libby reached out to touch her pearl earrings. "You like those?"

Libby kissed her and they hugged before Eli plucked his daughter away and handed her back to his mother. Libby didn't like that and started to protest.

"It's time for us to go, Brianna."

Her heart thudded because she'd seen the burning look of desire in his eyes.

"I'm ready."

Eli LED HER out of the room and they left the hotel through a side exit near their new truck. He helped her inside and drove them to a motel on the outskirts of town where there were individual chalet-style cabins nestled in the woods. He'd stopped by ahead of time to pick up the key and had dropped off food and snacks for them as well as their luggage.

Tomorrow they'd take a short trip to Helena for a few days, but tonight they weren't going anywhere. The fifty-degree temperature had melted the snow, making it easy to get around.

"I've been waiting for this for so long," he said as he helped her out of the truck. Then he scooped her up in his arms and carried her over the threshold of their cabin. Once the door was closed, he found her mouth and kissed her long after he'd put her down on the bed.

"We need to get you out of this divine wedding dress, but I don't want you to move."

"How about I just turn on my side and you can undo the buttons without either of us having to get up?"

"But I need to get up, if you follow my meaning."

"If you're talking about protection, I don't want to use any, but it's up to you. The last thing I want is for you to feel rushed into anything."

He kissed her neck. "Brianna…" She saw his tie and suit jacket fly through the air. That gave her his answer.

Somehow he managed to undo her dress. Before she knew it, they were entwined on the bed and her cowboy husband was loving her with a hunger she hadn't even imagined in her dreams. It was after midnight when he allowed her to breathe for a minute. "It's shocking how much I love you…how much I love making love with you, Eli."

"This is only the beginning, sweetheart. We've got the rest of our lives."

"The minister said this was a glorious day, but he didn't know how glorious."

He kissed a special spot. "So you like being married to me already."

"What if we'd never met?" she cried softly. "I can't imagine…"

"You don't have to, because we *did* meet, thanks to Roce. One of these days we'll do something nice for him, but right now all I want to do is make love to you for the rest of the night. You're the most gorgeous sight I have ever seen."

"You're my whole life, Eli. I can't believe I'm lucky enough to be your wife. You just don't know how happy I am. When I was in California I was so worried that something might go wrong. I don't know how I would have handled it if you'd decided to put off our marriage until Tessa was ready to deal with it."

He rolled her over on top of him. "Brianna—let's never talk about it again. She belongs in my past."

"I know."

"I'm going to work on making sure that you do. Give me your mouth again. It's life to me, don't you know that?"

If she didn't then, he managed to convince her so thoroughly that by late morning she truly felt they had become one flesh. She'd never really understood the term until now.

"Brianna? Do you think you want to drive to Helena today?" he whispered against her neck.

"You want the truth?"

He kissed the corners of her mouth. "Always."

"I don't want to go anywhere. I don't want to move from this bed."

He groaned. "How did I get so lucky to have you for my wife?"

"Let's just stay here until we have to go home."

"Mrs. Clayton, have you no shame?" he teased, nibbling on her lower lip.

"None. That's what you've done to me."

"I'm afraid I might have done something else to you."

"There's nothing I'd love more, but are you now wishing we'd used protection?"

"Of course not. I want a baby with you and hopefully more down the road. We haven't talked about it a lot, but I think it's important we give Libby a brother or sister soon. She's so used to being the center of attention that it will be good for her to be surrounded by siblings and have to learn to share."

"I agree. It's not only important, but siblings can be best friends. I'll always be thankful I grew up with a brother."

"You and me both."

She ran a finger over his compelling mouth. "If I do get pregnant right away, are you going to worry I might suffer postpartum depression after the delivery?"

"Not really. What happened to Tessa is quite rare. I refuse to let fear dominate our lives. I believe in us and our love."

Her eyes glazed over. "You're very brave. It's the quality that made you such a good bull rider. There isn't anything you can't do, is there? I love you so much."

"*You're* the one who's brave. Not every woman would have taken me on. Not every woman would have sacrificed her own needs and urged me to fight for my happiness and Libby's. Yet you hung in there."

"That's because you told me we have to operate

on faith that everything is going to be all right. We're in this forever."

"Forever. I love you. Come here to me, sweetheart."

* * * * *

Watch for MADE FOR THE RANCHER,
the next story in Rebecca Winters's miniseries
SAPPHIRE MOUNTAIN COWBOYS,
coming May 2017
only from Harlequin Western Romance!

Western Romance

Available February 7, 2017

#1629 THE TEXAS VALENTINE TWINS

Texas Legacies: The Lockharts
by Cathy Gillen Thacker

Estranged lovers Wyatt Lockhart and Adelaide Smyth have a one-night stand resulting in twin babies. While figuring out how to coparent they discover they are already married!

#1630 HER COWBOY LAWMAN

Cowboys in Uniform • by Pamela Britton

Sheriff Brennan Connelly, champion former bull rider, reluctantly agrees to help Lauren Danners's son learn to ride bulls. But his attraction to the much younger single mom is a distraction he doesn't need!

#1631 THE COWBOY'S VALENTINE BRIDE

Hope, Montana • by Patricia Johns

An IED sent Brody Mason home from Afghanistan, but he's determined to go back. There's nothing for him in Hope, Montana...except maybe Kaitlyn Harpe, the nurse who's helping him to walk again, ride again and maybe even love again.

#1632 A COWBOY IN HER ARMS

by Mary Leo

Callie Grant is stunned—the daughter of her ex and former best friend is in her kindergarten class! Widower Joel Darwood thinks what might be best for him and his child is Callie, if only he can convince her he's changed...

HWESTCNM0117